£2.50

The China Doll

Penelope was to spend the first Christmas after her marriage at the country home of her Great-Aunt Hermione, where she had lived as a child after the death of her parents. She looked forward to the traditionally peaceful holiday that she had known all her life. But before they left London, Vincent, her husband, gave her a present which was to prove a dominant factor in the events, tragic and terrifying, that followed. It was a small china doll.

During the weeks in which Penelope gradually realized that Vincent was in fact completely unlike the idea she had of him before their marriage, she met again Philip Torrington. An aspiring playwright, whom she had known all her life, he was now returned from a prolonged absence in the United States. Immediately disliking Vincent, Philip soon became suspicious of him. Yet he was unable to find a substantiation for his fears until it was almost too late to save Penelope.

The China Doll

MARGARET YORKE

CONTENTS

1

Vincent brought the doll home at five o'clock on Christmas Eve. It was small, less than a foot long, with a pale china face and dark hair cropped short. When it was made to stand, the opened eyes, fringed with thick lashes, were very blue. It wore a green velvet dress exactly the same colour as Penelope's new one, which had been bought at great expense from Chez Miriam at the corner of the mews only the week before.

'But it's exactly like me!' she exclaimed, inspecting it with mixed astonishment and pleasure. 'It hasn't even got a round face, like most dolls have!'

The little image stared back at her as she turned it about, gravely inspecting it. The chin was pointed, like her own, and the cheeks were without the rosy blush usually found in the complexions of dolls. Under the tiny green skirt there were layers of lace, and the feet were covered with little gold slippers.

'I know it's like you,' Vincent said. 'That's why, when I saw it, I bought it for you. Are you pleased with it?'

'Yes—yes, of course I am,' declared Penelope, stifling the small doubt that she began to feel. 'Thank you, darling.' She still looked at the doll, holding it in both hands: the likeness was uncanny. 'Where did you find it?' she asked.

'Oh, in a funny little shop just off the King's Road,' said Vincent. 'I just happened to notice it as I passed. Forgiven me for being late?'

'Oh —' Penelope made a face. 'I don't know—oh well, I suppose I must now,' she said, and smiled. 'But we must hurry. Aunt Hermione will worry if we're late.'

'It's always the same at Christmas,' Vincent said. 'Office parties and Christmas cheer among the staff. I really couldn't get away before.'

'Well, let's not waste any more time,' said Penelope quietly. She had been expecting him to come home at three o'clock, and when at last he had arrived, nearly two hours later, she had greeted him almost angrily. She had felt like this on more than one occasion in the last weeks; it frightened her and made her unhappy. She knew it was unreasonable to expect him to predict his movements down to the last minute; but after only three months of marriage she had begun to realize, though she did not allow herself to think about it, that when he was delayed beyond his expected time, her apprehension did not disappear with his return. Now she wrapped the doll up again in its tissue paper and put it back in the shiny white box in which it had travelled. She knew there was something missing in her thanks to her husband, and with an effort she put this right, kissing him quickly on the cheek.

Vincent took her by the shoulders and looked down at her quizzically. Deliberately he kissed her hard on the mouth. Trying not to do it obviously, Penelope moved out of his reach, still holding the box, and said, 'Shall I take it?'

'Why not?' Vincent replied. He was grinning at her, and she had begun to dread this now familiar, quite unmirthful smile. 'Your aunt might like to see it,' he went on.

Imperceptibly the doll had already become 'she'. Penelope laid the box down on a chair in the hall of their small house, where already her beaver coat and warm gloves were placed, waiting until at last Vincent agreed that they might leave.

'Very well,' she said. 'She'll have to go like this, there isn't room in my case. I had a job to close it.'

'Goodness knows why,' said Vincent. 'You won't need much down there, buried alive in the country, will you?' Without waiting for an answer he walked away, and called down to her as he mounted the stairs, 'I haven't much to collect. I won't be very long.'

Penelope did not remind him, as she longed to do, that if he had allowed her to do his packing he would now be ready to leave. She had already scolded him for being so late, and had coals of fire heaped upon her by his gift of the doll. She must not nag him. It was childish and unworthy, too, to feel disappointed in his choice of a present; she had so much hoped that he would give her the new evening bag for which she longed. It was silly of her to have misgivings about the doll; how clever Vincent had been to find it, many men would never have noticed such a thing, and it was certainly a highly original idea. Lots of people, Penelope knew, collected dolls of different sorts; some foreign ones were works of art, and valuable; perhaps she should do the same herself. She would not allow herself to face the idea that Vincent thought of her as still a child, and that his gift reflected this. She wandered away, into the sitting-room and sat down to wait. She had spent the afternoon polishing the furniture in it yet again, to fill in the time until Vincent came back from Automobile Kings, Ltd., where he worked. It was a bright little room on the first floor of the house, white painted, with red and white striped brocade curtains at the long windows, and green flowered cretonne covers on the four big arm-chairs that stood spaced out in a semi-circle round the electric fire. The bright metal glow gave Penelope no work, but it gave her small comfort with its warmth. She frowned, staring at it. She was so lucky: here they were, she and Vincent, married such a short time and owners of this converted maisonette which was equipped with every electrical aid to domesticity from a spin drier to the fire, and she was feeling dissatisfied because she missed the homeliness of glowing logs; and because, she admitted, she was bored. Every day Vincent left at nine o'clock for his office, and by half-past eleven she had scoured the house and was left without occupation till he came back in the evening, often as late as eight o'clock.

Oh well—better by far to have time on her hands than too much to do, Penelope decided, thinking of some of her friends. Perhaps after Christmas she might think seriously about taking a job again. Even if they didn't need the money now, they could save it for a holiday abroad later. She sighed. Really she was fortunate. While other people had to scrimp and scrape, Vincent was an executive of a prosperous motor company. It wasn't just a garage, she knew, but a luxury concern building special bodies and handling the very highest matters relating to car sales and hire. It sounded almost too grand to possess a service department for such humble tasks as greasing, and repairing punctures.

She got up, switched off the electric fire and went upstairs to the second floor to see if, after all, she would be allowed to help Vincent. He was in the bedroom, folding his red silk dressing-gown ready to be placed on the top of his filled suitcase. He looked up as she entered. His face, heavy and rather fleshy, wore a preoccupied expression, but it cleared when she came in and he smiled at her.

'Just ready,' he said, snapping the lid shut.

'Good.' She stood at the end of the bed, a thin, dark girl, very young, watching him solemnly out of her large blue eyes. Her small hands rested on the rolled mahogany end of the bed, and the narrow platinum wedding ring made a slight sound as it knocked against the wood. She looked down at it: it was still new enough to feel strange. She glanced up again at her husband. He had lifted the suitcase down from the bed and was watching her; his eyes, very light blue, were thoughtful.

'Well,' he said at last, with a smile, 'you'll know me again. What a stare!'

He was a tall man, well proportioned, with wide shoulders and small hands and feet. He had fair hair, so much plastered down to his skull that it had a greenish sheen in the electric light. Penelope thought wildly, 'I don't know him at all!' What was he thinking of now, watching her? That she was young and silly, when he was mature and wise? She had no idea what was going on behind the mask that was his face.

She was suddenly afraid. She loved him: of course she did: she had to love him. She moved blindly to him, and he put the suitcase down and embraced her patiently, until she seemed collected enough to return to the present, put on her coat and prepare to depart.

Like thousands of other people they were leaving London to spend Christmas in the country. Penelope had never spent it away from home before, and no one had suggested that although she was now married and had a house of her own she should depart from this custom. This morning she had woken as excited as the child she really was: she was going to Foxbourne St. Mary, back to Greyfriars and Great-Aunt Hermione who had brought her up after the tragically early death of both her parents, and from whose sheltering wing she had emerged only to go to school, and for the few months she had spent working in London before she met Vincent and was whisked off her feet into a whirlwind romance.

The car was parked below, in the mews. The short street was narrow, brightly lit by the lights shining from the windows of the row of small houses on one side, dark with the black wall of the warehouse that formed the other. Vincent carried the luggage downstairs, one suitcase in either hand and their two raincoats flung over his right shoulder. Penelope followed with a pile of gaily-wrapped parcels precariously balanced, and the white cardboard box containing her doll. Vincent opened the roomy boot and stowed it all neatly away inside. He was meticulous, and although there was ample room for everything, he stacked bags and parcels neatly beside one another like pieces in a jigsaw.

Soon they were moving slowly away down the street that glistened blackly after the day's rain. They passed the brightly-illuminated shop premises of Chez Miriam, where one white tulle evening dress alone in the window against a black background made a starkly dramatic display; and they passed the big old house on the corner where one gaunt tree hung, dripping, over rusting, green-painted railings. The car, a Vauxhall, was new; like all their possessions it had yet to acquire the clutter and stains of habit and use. Penelope had never driven it, although she held a licence. Vincent took it to work every day, and when they were together the question of who should drive never arose; he automatically always took the wheel.

Tonight the traffic was heavy, and most of it was going out of London. They waited in queues at lights, and sped at intervals more rapidly through clear spaces to the next congestion, but at last they reached the suburbs and were able to travel faster. Penelope snuggled down in her seat, the heater sending warm air circling round in front of her, and with a rug over her knees. On her lap was the box with the little doll inside, and her fur-gloved hands rested upon it.

Vincent drove with dedicated concentration. In the light from the street lamps and passing traffic his profile looked almost classical, with the straight nose and long jaw. He still wore a small moustache, relic of his Army days, a close-cut little tow-coloured bar above his thin mouth. The miles slid past: down the hill into Virginia Water, through Bagshot and Camberley, and past a spectral airfield where Penelope could see planes standing about like ghosts in the half-darkness, which was relieved by the brilliance from the illumined buildings.

Presently they turned off the main road and began to travel along lanes, narrow tunnels walled with high, untrimmed hedges, through hamlets and beneath railway bridges, until they reached Foxbourne St. Mary. Penelope felt a surge of excitement: she was coming home. Up the hill they went, round the corner by the church, a hundred yards to the left, and there were the big white gates, always open unless cows were being driven down the road.

Vincent changed gear. There was a splutter of gravel as the tyres crunched on the loose stones by the entrance. The car moved on along the drive, under the overhanging branches of the big trees, up the slope to where the house stood on a little rise with a wide gravel sweep in front of it, and neatly-trimmed yew hedges hiding the terraced garden that fell away, down the hill, to the stream where Penelope as a child had often fished.

Great-Aunt Hermione had been listening for them. She was at the open door before they were out of the car. Framed in the lighted doorway she waited for them, leaning on her stick, and Penelope hurried towards her. There were tears in her eyes: she was home. She was safe.

2

At once they were engulfed by the Greyfriars atmosphere, with its familiar smell of furniture polish and wood fires, mixed now with the tangy fragrance of chrysanthemums that were massed in a tub in the hall. As always, a big bunch of mistletoe, secured by a scarlet ribbon, hung below the light, and as Vincent bent to kiss Great-Aunt Hermione's papery cheek, with a smile she moved beneath it.

Now they were all laughing. It was warm in the house, and cheerful. There was holly in swathes bound to the thick beams; there were dozens of Christmas cards standing in ranks in every available place, on the tables, the cupboards, and even on the bookshelves; there was a decanter and sherry glasses on the low coffee table near the fire; and there was, as there had always been, a Christmas tree with coloured lights and the same little blonde fairy doll, dressed in silver, with wand outstretched, on the topmost branch.

'Oh, Vincent! My little doll! I left it in the car,' Penelope said.

'I'll fetch it,' said Vincent, who had walked to the fire and was rubbing his hands in the warmth from the blaze. He turned at once.

'Cartwright will bring in your luggage, Vincent,' said Great-Aunt Hermione. 'He heard you arrive. He'll be out there now.'

'Ah, good. I'll give him a hand,' said Vincent. 'Penelope's worrying about her first present—we've stolen a march on the date and she's had one already.' He turned back and went out of the room again.

'What's this, my pet? A doll, did you say?' Aunt Hermione moved round and looked at Penelope.

The girl nodded. 'Yes. Wait till you see it. Vincent gave it to me this evening. I'm sorry we're so late, Aunt Hermione, were you worrying? Vincent couldn't get away from the office. I do hope dinner won't be spoilt.'

'Don't you fret, we've got a casserole tonight—I thought you might get held up in the traffic, or the roads might be icy, so Queenie and I planned something that wouldn't spoil. In any case, she wanted to hold herself in reserve for tomorrow, and it wouldn't do for us to overtax our systems beforehand.'

Penelope laughed. She stretched out her arms, still wearing her dark beaver coat, and sighed. 'Oh, it's good to be home,' she said.

'Happy?' The old lady was looking at her shrewdly. She was thin, but so she had always been: it was natural to be pleased at coming home again after her first months as a housewife. It was all still new, and she had not settled down yet. There was no time for her to answer, but her eyes were clear and her young brow smooth, and as Vincent came back into the room carrying the small white box that contained her doll, balanced on top of a pile of Christmas parcels, she moved towards him.

Vincent laid the heap of presents down on a chair and then gave her the doll. Penelope opened the box and held it out for her aunt to see: in its nest of white paper the absurd reflection of herself was revealed.

Great-Aunt Hermione was startled. She took the doll out of the box and inspected it.

'But how amazing, Penny,' she exclaimed. 'It's exactly like you. Vincent, where did you find such a thing? It's charming.'

Vincent, busy arranging the other parcels in a safe stack, repeated the story of how he had seen the doll in a shop window.

'Well, how delightful,' said Aunt Hermione, putting it back in the box again. 'It's the most remarkable coincidence, what in my young days we would have called a charming conceit.' She handed it back to Penelope, who was hovering in a vague way between her and Vincent.

'We'd better tidy for dinner,' said the girl hesitantly.

'Yes, run along,' said Great-Aunt Hermione. 'Dinner won't be long. Have your sherry when you come down.'

Penelope left the room and went upstairs. Vincent glanced across at the old lady in her crimson velvet dress and smiled. Then he followed his wife.

Their suitcases were already waiting in the room that had been Penelope's before her marriage. Great-Aunt Hermione had furnished it again to make room for Vincent, but there was still Penelope's own little walnut dressing-table in the corner by the window. It felt reassuringly familiar as she opened the drawers to put away her handkerchiefs, lipstick and powder where they had always lived. Vincent was padding about taking everything out of his own bag and arranging his possessions tidily in the tall chest of drawers that had once belonged to Great-Uncle Cedric, the now dead husband of Great-Aunt Hermione.

'The old lady seems well,' said Vincent, finding his ivory-backed hairbrushes and slicking them both rhythmically over his hair.

'Yes.' Penelope had found some shoes, bronze court ones with slender, tapering heels, and was changing her fur-lined boots for them. 'I expect she's been quite quiet lately.'

Vincent laughed. 'I wonder—I don't think she could be really quiet—too fond of her friends,' he said.

'Well, since Dr Torrington told her to slow up I think she has been taking things more gently,' Penelope insisted. 'I'll have a chat with Queenie later and see what she thinks about it.'

'Poor old toot,' said Vincent briefly.

Penelope wanted to ask him not to call Great-Aunt Hermione a poor old toot, but again she controlled the impulse. Vincent had only known her for a few months, possibly to him she did seem a funny old thing. When they went downstairs again she tried to be objective and imagine how he felt, a comparative stranger here, in what was to her, home.

Great-Aunt Hermione had been an actress before she met and married Cedric Vandyk in 1915. Though wounded several times, he had survived the War, and gone on to make a fortune out of biscuits, in middle age. Then he had sold his business and retired. He and his wife were a well-suited pair, both cheerful extroverts who had enjoyed the money that they had, spending a lot of it but wisely investing most, and in spite of death duties Great-Aunt Hermione, in her widowhood, was affluent. Three years ago Cedric had died, after an operation, all very quickly, very neatly, without much pain or suffering; but Great-Aunt Hermione, although she carried on bravely, had died a little too, and had welcomed the advent of Vincent as a chance to relinquish her last responsibility. She tried to keep her zest for life; indeed, as Vincent guessed, her days were pleasant to her, but at the end of each one, alone, existence seemed a little pointless.

Penelope thought her aunt looked pale in the light of the candles on the dinner table, but she talked cheerfully, blue eyes twinkling, her mottled old hands steady and her hearing as acute as the young people's. Vincent sat on her right at the long oak table; and because she had always, throughout her long life, enjoyed the society of men, she took pleasure in his company. It was good that Penelope had chosen someone rather older than herself, mature enough to look after her, and to protect her childish vulnerability in the harsh world where Great-Aunt Hermione, more brave, had enjoyed battling. The child would grow up soon enough; Vincent would, she hoped, let the process be a gentle one. She had not felt any anxiety at the swiftness of the romance between the two: her own had been a lightning, instant experience which she had never once regretted; and whilst aware that less fortunate conditions sometimes prevailed she saw no reason to doubt that Penelope, in her different way, might still be blessed with the same good fortune.

During dinner Cartwright, wearing his white jacket, waited at table. He was a small, silent-footed man with a round, bald head, who had served Great-Uncle Cedric as his batman during the First World War, assisted him with air raid warden's duties during the second, and between these spells and after them ministered to him in all possible ways to ensure his physical comfort. To aid the process, when help in the house was hard to get in the 1940's, he had married Queenie Castle, the improbably-christened buxom daughter of the landlord of The Feathers, renowned throughout the county for her cooking, and had added her to the establishment. Thus well catered for, the household had since never lacked for bodily comfort.

Cartwright had not placed Vincent yet: a different type, very, from the Colonel, as he always liked to think of his late master; but his shoes were good and well polished, his luggage travel-stained but costly: he must be sound, and he was certainly able to look after little Miss Penny, though perhaps someone nearer her own age would have made her laugh more. Still, fifteen years divided him from his Queenie, and in the privacy of their own rooms at the end of the house they laughed a lot, and most rumbustiously, unknown to the outside world. Changing the plates, Cartwright confided to Queenie that Penelope was quiet, but no doubt she was tired after the journey down, and she looked as pretty as a picture.

Coffee mousse followed the casserole, and then Great-Aunt Hermione led the way back into the drawing-room. It was large, with big, old-fashioned furniture, some of it very good, and several valuable paintings in heavy gilt frames on the walls.

'Who's coming tomorrow night?' Penelope asked, curling up on the hearthrug in front of the fire like a little kitten. 'Same band as before?'

'Yes, my pet,' said Great-Aunt Hermione. 'Major Tompkins—your friend, Vincent, poor man, he must be lonely—and Kitty Francis—why don't those two get married? And Dr and Mrs Torrington, and Philip. He's back from America.'

'Philip?' Vincent looked up as Cartwright came in with the coffee tray.

'Philip Torrington—their son and my godson,' said Great-Aunt Hermione. 'He's a journalist—he wants to write plays, but the poor boy has to earn his living. He's been in America for the last three years working on various papers out there to get experience.'

'Oh, how nice to see Philip again,' said Penelope. 'I didn't know he was coming back.'

If Great-Aunt Hermione had one regret it was that her godson, Philip Torrington, to whom she was devoted, had not returned in time to meet the grown-up Penelope before Vincent came upon the scene, for a match between them had been her dream. But he was young and impetuous, red-haired and impatient; Vincent, with his slower brain and wider experience was perhaps the wiser choice: he was successful and attentive, where Philip, who was still making his way, might be thoughtless and selfish. Philip and Penelope had been great friends as children; now they might well have grown too far apart to find a common interest.

'Church in the morning, of course,' said Penelope sleepily. 'Then lunch, a walk, and the Queen. Or the Queen, and then a walk.' She looked at Vincent. 'That's how it's always been,' she said.

'Of course, sweetheart,' said Vincent, smiling at her. He had lighted a cigarette, and sat sideways in the large wing chair, his head against the back of it, looking down at her. She appeared very small and defenceless sitting there on the patterned Persian rug by the hearth, her shoes kicked off and her small feet tucked up under her skirt. Her body was so slight that it looked as if a hand could crush it. He flexed his fingers, holding his square left hand out and squinting at it appraisingly. Strong fair hairs covered the back of it; the tips of his fingers were blunt and stubby. He looked down at his wife again, and meeting his expression she felt her face begin to flame.

Later, when she was sitting up in bed, like a child waiting to be tucked up by its nanny for the night, listening for Vincent's return from the bath, her glance fell on the mirror. Someone had taken the little doll from its box: standing up on its two small feet, it had been placed on the mantelpiece and reflected in the glass, looking at her, was the little miniature of her own face, large-eyed and pale, and apprehensive.

3

The damp mugginess of the past few days had gone by morning, and with the clearer air there was a corresponding increase in the tempo of life. Penelope's eyes, large and very dark this morning, shone with excitement as she ate a plateful of porridge. Vincent, deploring the practice, which was not one she maintained in Kensington, tackled fried eggs, sausages, tomatoes and fried bread, and listened while she told him who would be in church, and where the Meet would be tomorrow, and how she wondered if Great-Aunt Hermione would like the dressing-gown that was her present, as if he had not heard it all a dozen times before. Great-Aunt Hermione had breakfast in bed, because of her heart, as she did every day, but this morning she was down early because it was Christmas and there were parcels to unwrap before they went off to church.

Vincent drove them in the Vauxhall, down the road to the corner and round to the church, for Great-Aunt Hermione was not allowed to walk very far. They passed Cartwright and his Queenie walking neatly along, side by side, he small and spare, she plump and exuberant, her wide hips tight against the woollen cloth of her beaver-collared coat, and on her hands the new fur gloves that Penelope had chosen with so much care. Cartwright was wearing his spotted silk scarf, also a gift from herself and Vincent, so they must both have been pleased with their presents.

As for herself, she could not believe it. It was pinned to her suit lapel now, the lovely brooch, small diamonds set in the shape of a leaf in platinum. She had nearly refused to put on her overcoat, wanting the present that Vincent had given her to be seen by everyone. How dull by comparison the cashmere waistcoat that she had given him, but he was wearing that too.

O come all ye faithful, they sang loudly, and soon came the familiar lesson from Isaiah, read no longer by Great-Uncle Cedric but by General Carne from the Manor.

Vincent could not find the Psalm. With a shock Penelope realized that they had, apart from their wedding, never been to church together before. From the corner of her eye she saw him hunting unobtrusively about in his prayer book for the right place. Even if he seldom went to church, school, surely had made him familiar with the lay-out of the prayer book?

He seemed to know *Hark the Herald Angels,* though, and *While Shepherds Watched;* his light tenor voice could plainly be heard in both, and she was reassured.

They went back to the Manor for sherry with General and Mrs Carne. It was in their house that Penelope had first met Vincent, not so very long before. Great-Aunt Hermione, sitting on the chesterfield talking to the General, looked tired, and Penelope would not let them linger because there was still so much of the day ahead.

Lunch was cold—pork pie, ham and salad, with celery and beetroot, for the kitchen was stripped ready for action to prepare the Christmas dinner. Afterwards Great-Aunt Hermione went to lie down on her bed.

'I'm worried about her,' Penelope told Vincent, as they sat in front of the blazing fire. 'Queenie says Dr Torrington can't really do anything to help, except give her various pills. She's just—wearing out slowly. It's horrible.'

'She's lived a long time,' said Vincent. 'I don't suppose she wants to go on much longer.' His face was set, looking at the fire, a cigarette in his hand.

'She'd hate to be a complete invalid,' said Penelope. 'But all the same —' she fell silent. This was depressing talk for Christmas Day. 'Let's go for a walk,' she said, getting up and holding a hand out towards him.

It was very damp outside, and in the silence of the windless air drops of moisture fell with sharp plops from the trees and the hedges on to the ground. They walked briskly down the lane for half-a-mile or more, meeting no one except a small boy busy riding his brand new tricycle, and then they returned to Greyfriars, just in time for the Queen's broadcast. Great-Aunt Hermione had recently bought a television set, because she could no longer go out and about as much as she liked. Now she spent hours watching controversial programmes and plays and freely criticizing what she saw. She came downstairs in time to watch the relay from Sandringham, and the Cartwrights came from the kitchen too, to see it.

Great-Aunt Hermione sat on the sofa, leaning forward on her stick, intently watching the serene and lovely face of her Sovereign. Queenie and her husband sat on small chairs further away from the screen. Penelope curled up on the floor, and Vincent sprawled in an arm-chair. During the Anthem everyone, even Great-Aunt Hermione, stood upright. Cartwright, an old soldier, remained stiffly at attention, hands at the seams of his trousers and his head erect, eyes to the front. Queenie kept her arms crossed over her ample bosom. Penelope folded her hands behind her back.

Great-Aunt Hermione, swaying slightly on her stick, smiled as she saw their different positions, and frowned a little when she noticed that Vincent stood with his feet apart, leaning against the wall, a cigarette still in one hand.

Afterwards Penelope said, 'Do you remember that game we used to play, "Christmas Cards"? What a pity there aren't more of us, we might have done it, but three isn't really enough.'

'A silly game, dear,' said Great-Aunt Hermione with a smile.

'The right sort of foolishness for a day like this,' Penelope said. She turned to Vincent. 'You collect up all the Christmas cards you can, and deal them out to all the players. Then you take it in turns to play, calling out suits, like "Father Christmas", or "Holly", and everyone has to play a card with that sort of picture on it. Whoever the majority votes to have put down the best card wins the trick. The fun is in knowing whether to play your picture of a church for "Churches", or keep it in case someone calls "Holy". It's fun.'

'Sounds terrific,' said Vincent. Great-Aunt Hermione glanced at him again. His face was impassive; there was no way of knowing really whether he mocked.

Later she went to her room, and Penelope followed to see if she could help her change.

'Look at my new dress—what do you think of it?' asked the old lady. On a hanger outside her big, old-fashioned wardrobe hung a richly-brocaded dress, gold, embroidered with flowers in every colour. It was magnificent, the sort of dress which, as a young woman Great-Aunt Hermione had often worn, both she and the dress lending each other dramatic dignity.

'Oh, it's gorgeous! What heavenly material,' Penelope exclaimed. She examined it. 'Where did you get it?'

'Wrote to Madame Eugenie, as usual,' said Great-Aunt Hermione, chuckling. 'My statistics still seem the same, it fits beautifully.'

'I can't think why you won't come up and stay with us for a week or two,' said Penelope. 'Then you could have a fitting, get your hair decently done, and so on. Shall I switch on the fire for you?'

'Please, dear.' Great-Aunt Hermione had seated herself in front of her dressing-table and was peering into the mirror. 'I'm getting too old to enjoy the shops and the noise, and I manage quite well like this, but I will come and stay in the spring, my pet, when you've had more time to get used to your Vincent.'

Penelope bent to plug in the electric fire and pressed down the switch.

'I'm used to him now,' she protested, straightening, and then, meeting the wise old eyes in the mirror, 'Well, no, perhaps not quite, but I'll always find him exciting, won't I?'

'I hope you find him comfortable too,' said her aunt.

Penelope laughed. 'You make him sound like a pair of shoes,' she said.

'Well, he should be,' said Great-Aunt Hermione. 'A support, complement and stimulus that you would hate to be without.'

Penelope cried, 'He's so generous, look at my lovely brooch.'

'Very beautiful, my pet,' said Great-Aunt Hermione. 'He must be doing well. I'm glad, my dear.' She had taken off her rings, and now ran her comb through her thick hair, frowning. 'I wanted a chat with you, Penny. Just see if the tongs are hot, will you?'

Penelope crossed to the open fireplace, where on the stone hearth stood an electric fire. It was one of the swivelling type, and it was turned upwards so that its bright glow pointed towards the ceiling. Resting across the metal guard over the elements was a pair of curling tongs. She bent down and gingerly lifted them off, using an old felt glove that lay beside the fire to protect her fingers from the metal handles.

'I wish you wouldn't do this,' grumbled Penelope, handing them unwillingly to the old lady.

Great-Aunt Hermione accepted the tongs, and tested their temperature by opening them, and then closing them round a piece of tissue paper. There was a slight scorching smell, and she nodded in a satisfied way, withdrew the paper and then began to thrust the tongs into her hair, deepening the corrugations among her chestnut locks. Her hair as a girl had been her chief vanity; thick, brilliant and wavy, she had treasured it, and when its colour began to fade and its wave to diminish she resorted to artifice to restore both. After Great-Uncle Cedric's death the secrecy of her operations had gradually decreased, and now it was known so openly that the bottle of dye stood blatantly on the bathroom shelf, and the tongs lived permanently across the guard of the electric fire waiting for their daily ritual.

'You'll burn yourself,' Penelope went on, watching while the waves were clamped firmly like ploughed furrows into the still luxuriant hair. 'Or give yourself a shock,' she added. 'I'll see if I can find you a better way of heating the tongs—meths or something.'

'Oh, I've tried that—such a bother. This is far the easiest way,' said Great-Aunt Hermione. 'No trouble at all, and the fire is cosy.'

'It's like an oven,' said Penelope, frowning. 'You bad old thing, you're quite warm enough with the radiators, you don't want this too.'

'Ah, your blood is young,' said her aunt. 'Wait till you're my age, then you'll understand about thin old blood and thick old arteries.'

Penelope chuckled. 'Well, I suppose it's no good trying to make you mend your ways now,' she said.

'No good at all,' agreed Great-Aunt Hermione. 'But there is something, Penny, a change I do want to make. It concerns you, and I want to talk to you about it.'

'Oh? What is it?' The girl sat down on the large four-poster bed. 'Tell me.'

'It's about my will,' said Great-Aunt Hermione. 'As you know, you are my only heir. Uncle Cedric and I had no children, and your mother was his only surviving relation after your uncles were killed in the war. I wouldn't dream of altering his intention that you should inherit his fortune, which is still considerable, but now there's Philip.'

'In what way?' Penelope was embarrassed. She did not like to think of dead men's shoes.

'Well, you know what a dear he is, and he's my godson. I think he shows great promise as a writer: some of his plays have a real sense of theatre, but he can't concentrate on them when he has to earn his living. His parents can't help him—in any case they are disappointed because he hasn't taken up medicine like his father. But Philip wouldn't want their help even if they could give it. I want to make him financially independent so that he can give up journalism and do his real work.'

'But of course you must!' Penelope blushed. 'Leave him all your money—I've got Vincent, and anyway you won't die for years and years.'

Great-Aunt Hermione smiled. 'I won't live for ever, child,' she said. 'And I don't want to go on till I'm just a worry to you. You'll still be wealthy one day, darling, but less wealthy than you might have been. You won't feel badly about it?'

'Of course not—let Philip have it all, I don't need it,' cried Penelope proudly.

'You'll be able to use it, my dear,' said the old lady gently. She had been watching the girl through the mirror while they talked, but now she turned slowly and stiffly on the stool and faced her. 'I intend to leave Philip a quarter of my capital. I knew you'd understand and agree, but I wanted to explain to you, so that you wouldn't be hurt when my will is proved.'

'Don't let's talk about such gloomy things,' said Penelope gruffly. She got up from the bed and went over to her aunt. 'Hurry up and get dressed and be a bit cheerful,' she admonished, hugging her. 'I'm going to change now.'

Vincent was ready, wearing his dinner jacket, when she entered their room a moment later. He did look handsome, so tall and soldierly. Of course, he had been in the army, she knew, for years and years. He had stayed in it after the war and served in Korea and in Africa. It was while he was staying with Major Tompkins, a former brother officer, who also lived in Foxbourne St. Mary, that she had met him last spring at the Carnes' cocktail party.

'Oh, darling, you're ready early,' she exclaimed.

'Where have you been?' he asked. He was transferring a little heap of loose change from the top of the chest of drawers where he had laid it earlier into his trouser pocket.

'I've been having a gossip with Aunt Hermione and helping her curl her hair—you know, with the tongs, how she always does, I told you, though you're supposed to think it's natural. But she doesn't pretend so much since Uncle Cedric died.'

'What were you talking about?' Vincent enquired idly.

'Oh, money and things. Us. It was rather horrid. I don't like to think of her dying,' said Penelope with a shiver. 'She wants to change her will and leave something to Philip Torrington, so that he can chuck the newspapers and write plays all the time.'

'Oh? Is she going to?' Vincent looked up.

'Oh yes, rather. Of course I told her to go ahead, because I've got you,' said Penelope, undoing the zip of her dress. She began to pull it off over her head.

'Yes, of course you have, my sweet,' said Vincent, helping her. He drew it up like a tea cosy, and she stood in her petticoat before him. He bent to kiss her, the dress bundled over his arm. 'Of course you've always got me,' he murmured.

When he had gone she sat on the bed to change her stockings. The little doll had been moved, and now lay on top of her pillow, hands by its sides, eyes closed, as if asleep. Abruptly Penelope picked it up and turned it over on its face, where it remained until Queenie Cartwright came up later to turn down the bed and found it. Clucking in surprise, the good soul sat it up on the dressing-table, propped against the mirror, where Penelope would be sure to see it when she came to brush her hair.

4

Mrs cartwright kept three goldfish in a bowl that stood on the kitchen window-sill. Round and round they swam, gills flapping rhythmically and mouths gasping as they begged through the thick glass for the ants' eggs she sparingly allowed them. In summer, when the fields were dry, she fetched weed for them from the stream, and they lived for months in a torrid, semi-tropical forest, scraping against the fronds and playing silent, stately games of hide-and-seek among the greenery. Queenie alleged that it soothed her nerves to watch them, but in fact unruly nerves were something alien to her robust temperament. She enjoyed the spectacle of the fishes circling monotonously round in much the same way that she enjoyed the first snowdrops, young lambs, a fattening pig, or any other satisfying manifestation of life.

She was in her element in the midst of Christmas dinner preparations. Shining saucepans for the sprouts and the sauces were ranged upon the table; the turkey, not so enormous as to be tough, but a plump and succulent hen bird certain to be tender, and chosen earlier in the year by Queenie herself from among those who spent their brief life in the turkey parlour at Butts Farm up the lane, was in the oven. At intervals Queenie opened the oven door to baste it, and rich, mouth-watering smells escaped as she did so.

Cartwright had laid the table. All the best silver gleamed on the dark, polished oak; and tall red candles rose from a bed of white and silvered holly leaves painted by Kitty Francis, a maiden lady of uncertain age who lived in a cottage at the end of the village and painted papier-maché trays and bric-a-brac, and sometimes wrote poetry. Snowy table-napkins, folded intricately like water-lilies, waited in each place. Cartwright surveyed the room: all was prepared. It gave him pleasure to see everything so perfectly arranged, with nothing forgotten—the heavy old Georgian salts and peppers shining, the chairs all placed and the deep red curtains drawn in the warm room.

He went into the drawing-room and made up the fire, plumped up the cushions and tidied the chairs back into their proper positions. He emptied the ashtrays filled with Vincent's stubs—for neither Penelope nor her aunt smoked—and then brought in the tray of drinks. Finally, satisfied that man could do no more, he returned to the kitchen, took off his spotless jacket, and sat down with his feet up to watch the ever-pleasing spectacle of Queenie at her work until the front-door bell should ring.

'See that Penny has a nice piece off the breast, Bert,' instructed Queenie, her bare plump forearms quivering as, stooping, she pulled the heavy roasting tin half out of the oven the better to baste the bird. A spot of fat fell on the shelf and spat, sizzling, into dryness. 'She's so skinny, that child.'

'Wonder if he'll carve?' mused Cartwright.

'Who? Vincent? What a name—did you ever hear the like?' Penelope's husband had yet to win his spurs below stairs.

'Um. Him. The doctor's done it the last two years, since the old Colonel was taken,' said Cartwright pensively. He still missed his master.

'He's the one, if you ask me, to carry on.' Queenie closed the oven door emphatically. 'Sort of ready trained for the job, isn't he? Wonder he doesn't bring his own knives with him.' She turned to inspect the pudding, steaming steadily in its bowl. A tray of mince pies, golden-brown and warm, dusted lightly with sugar, stood at the side of the stove, keeping hot. To Queenie her kitchen smelt like paradise.

'Well, our Penny seems happy enough, pretty as a picture even if she is thin,' said Cartwright.

'All the same, I'm sorry young Philip didn't have a look-in,' said Queenie, beginning to beat up the hard sauce. 'I always had a soft spot for that one, red hair and all, and what pranks they got up to as kids. He was always fond of Penny.'

'Lovely brooch he gave her, all the same—Vincent.' Queenie and her husband always referred thus intimately in private to the addition to the family.

'Mm. Must have cost a bit.' Queenie's powerful wrists were working hard, beating the butter and sugar together with the easy skill of years. 'Must think a lot of her, spending all that.'

'Maybe. Still—if he can afford it he'd be mean not to, wouldn't he?' enquired Cartwright.

'Oh—I dunno,' said Queenie. 'I always thought more of that bunch of wild violets you gave me when we got engaged than anything you spent your money on since, and you aren't mean, I will say,' she conceded.

Cartwright blushed at this reminder of his former romanticism. He was spared from the need to reply by the sound of the front-door bell. He struggled back into his short white coat and went off, muttering, 'Someone's early, I haven't heard our lot come down yet, not seven o'clock by any means.'

It was Philip Torrington who stood on the front-door step. He was a small, rather thin young man, with very bright amber-coloured eyes, surprising in his fair face which had the clear pallor common among redheaded people who escape being carroty. His overcoat collar was turned up round his ears, and his hair was beaded with little drops of moisture from the damp air. A small green open M.G. two-seater, with its hood down could dimly be seen drawn up by the hedge.

'Why, Mr Philip!' Cartwright was pleased to see him.

' 'Evening, Cartwright. How are you?' The young man's hand shot out as he entered the house, and he shook the manservant's vigorously.

'Oh, very well, sir, thank you. No need to ask you how you are.' Cartwright peered out into the night wondering where the rest of the Torringtons were.

'Oh, I'm the first, I suppose,' said Philip. 'I've been up to see General Carne, and came straight on here. Mother and Father are coming separately—I expect I'm a bit early.'

'Yes, you are, Mr Philip,' said Cartwright. 'Mrs Vandyk isn't down yet, but I don't expect she'll be long.' He helped Philip off with his heavy tweed overcoat, and the young man ran a hand over his thick, dark red hair, smoothing it down.

'How's Queenie?'

'Oh, very well, thank you, sir,' said Cartwright. 'She'll be pleased to see you, if you could just pop out some time.'

'I certainly will,' said Philip. 'Better later, eh? She'll be up to her eyes now with stuffing and so forth.'

'Well, she is busy,' Cartwright agreed. 'Perhaps after dinner sometime, if you can slip away.' He was guiding Philip towards the drawing-room. 'Mr Dereham is down, I think, I caught a glimpse of him as I came to let you in,' he said.

Philip raised his sandy eyebrows. 'Penny's husband?'

Cartwright nodded. His round face became inscrutable.

'All right?' Philip had known Cartwright since he was a little boy.

'It's early days, Mr Philip,' was the non-commital reply.

But the drawing-room was empty when the door was opened.

'Well, I must have imagined I saw him,' muttered Cartwright, looking puzzled. 'Anyway, they won't be long, sir,' he added, his mode of address for Philip fluctuating with every sentence.

'I'll pop up and see Mrs Vandyk—I haven't seen her since I got back from America—I'd like to have a word with her and be put in the picture about Penelope and so on,' said Philip. 'She will be nearly ready, by now, won't she?'

'Oh, yes, Mr Philip. She'll just be putting on her jewellery and that,' said Cartwright. 'You go up, she'll be pleased.'

Philip bounded up the stairs, two at a time, and strode along the passage to the old lady's door, where he knocked and was told to enter.

Great-Aunt Hermione was standing admiring herself in her long mirror. The gold-embroidered dress hung straight to the floor like a mandarin's coat. The neck was high, and the wide sleeves fell to just below the elbow. Her thick hair, stiffly waved, looked curiously artificial round her pink, kind old face, but the effect was most striking.

'Phew!' Philip whistled. 'How splendid you are, my aunt!'

'Philip! Oh, my dear boy, come and kiss me!' Great-Aunt Hermione flung her arms wide and stood waiting for him.

Philip went over to her at once, hugged her hard and kissed her soundly on both cheeks, almost lifting her bodily off the floor as he did so.

'Oh, that was nice!' Aunt Hermione released him at last. 'I don't often get a kiss from a nice young man these days, Philip.'

He laughed. 'Doesn't what's-his-name—Dereham—doesn't he kiss you?' he asked.

'A duty peck,' said Aunt Hermione. And to tell you the truth, though I'm much attached to him, I'd blush at more,' she declared.

'I don't believe you, you wicked old lady,' said Philip blithely. He sat down, as Penelope had earlier done, on the edge of the large bed, and Aunt Hermione's frail old heart warmed at the sight of him, healthy, young and vital. 'But tell me about him, all the same. I must be in the picture. Wasn't it all rather quick?'

Aloud, Philip would never acknowledge the horrified shock which the news, contained casually in a letter from his mother, had been: Penelope was only eighteen; he had not seen her for years and had not realized that she was in fact old enough to marry until it had happened.

'Well, it was I suppose, but Cedric and I married like that,' Aunt Hermione defended herself. She pulled her dress straight after Philip's embrace, smoothing her hands down her well-corseted sides. 'They met in the spring, Vincent was staying with Fred Tompkins at the time. They're old Army friends, and that's a recommendation in itself. Of course, he's a lot older than Penny, but then she's had no real father, she needs an older husband, and he's doing very well, he's a director of some big car place in the West End—Automobile Kings, near the Strand.'

'Hm!' Philip was impressed. 'A prosperous bloke, is he?'

'Very,' said Aunt Hermione. And Penny's a lucky girl,' she added firmly. 'She was playing about in some foolish job at the time, working for a house-agent; it wasn't at all the best thing for her. So I was glad when Vincent married her four months after they'd met, and took her out of it. A girl like Penny needs a husband to look after her.'

Philip refrained from saying that she might have managed to endure a little longer without one: the deed was done. Meanwhile the old lady went on speaking.

'They're very happy, they've got a dear little house in Kensington, and Vincent's just given her the most beautiful diamond brooch for Christmas.'

'Well, if she's happy and he's a decent chap that's all we really want for Penny, isn't it?' said Philip, and wondered why he felt forlorn.

'Of course it is,' said Aunt Hermione. Then she confessed frankly, 'Mind you, I once hoped something might happen between you and Penny, my two favourite people now that Cedric's gone, but you know each other too well.'

'I don't know Penny at all now,' Philip demurred. 'She was a schoolgirl when I last saw her.' He could see her in imagination, small and thin, able to quote Shakespeare by the yard but in all other ways the despair of her instructresses.

'She hasn't really changed,' Aunt Hermione said. 'And how happy I am to have you both here under my roof for my last Christmas.'

Philip was shocked. He stood up.

'Dearest aunt, you'll have lots more,' he protested. He peered at her round, pink face. Perhaps that colour owed more to art than nature.

'I don't want any more,' she said. 'I've had all I want. Penny's safe, and I've lasted long enough to see you again, my dear boy, and what a treat you are for sore eyes too.' She chuckled.

Then she continued: 'I miss my dear Cedric, and I can't get about much now. Your father can't replace my poor old worn-out heart, and I don't want to be just another crock. Penny's settled with her Vincent, and you'll be settled too when I've seen my solicitors next week. That's all I want to do now. I'm leaving you a little legacy, Philip, not a lot, but enough to live on without worry, in a modest way, while you write. Now don't protest, Penny knows and agrees, and we both want you to be able to do your scribbling without thinking about your bread and butter. I believe in your ability, boy, and one day you'll write a play that will justify me, but not if you're posting about all over the globe searching for scoops.'

This was hardly how Philip would have described his journalistic activities of the past few years, but it was true that his various columns had absorbed almost all his energies and concentration.

'Penelope will have plenty, and besides, Vincent will look after her,' Great-Aunt Hermione added.

Philip was nonplussed. He rubbed the carpet with his toe, a gesture the old lady remembered him making as a child whenever he was embarrassed.

'Now I must go downstairs,' she said. 'The others will wonder where I am.' She crossed to her dressing-table once more and dabbed an extra spot of powder on her nose. Then her glance fell on the curling tongs, lying where she had left them earlier after using them, on a crumpled, singed piece of paper. She picked them up.

'Just pop these on the fire, Philip, there's a dear boy,' she said, holding them out to him.

Philip took them. 'Whatever are they?' he asked.

'Curling tongs for my hair,' said Great-Aunt Hermione absently. 'Lay them on top of the guard, Philip, then they'll be ready to heat up nicely when I switch it on in the morning.' She patted her head. 'This isn't natural any more.'

Philip had known for years that Great-Aunt Hermione's hair owed its colour to a bottle, but the tongs were new to him. He laid them carefully across the bars of the fire, standing in front of it and stooping down.

'Isn't it dangerous?' he asked.

'Oh no—I've been doing it for years,' said Great-Aunt Hermione.

Philip frowned. Metal on metal. But as she said, she'd been doing it for years.

'Come.' Great-Aunt Hermione held out her arm. 'Take me downstairs.'

5

Penelope was sitting in one of the big wing arm-chairs when they entered the drawing-room arm-in-arm a few minutes later. She was alone. She rose at once, in a quick unfolding movement filled with sudden grace.

Philip halted on the threshold of the room, staring at her, and bringing Great-Aunt Hermione also to an abrupt standstill.

'It's Penelope, Philip,' Great-Aunt Hermione explained unnecessarily, tugging him onwards.

'Yes, I know,' said Philip earnestly. He continued to stare, but dropped Great-Aunt Hermione's arm unceremoniously and advanced across the room.

'Hullo, Philip.' Penelope was unaware that the passage of three years had greatly changed her appearance from what Philip remembered, and was delighted to find that he seemed quite unaltered. They shook hands formally, and it was pleasant for her to meet eyes nearly on a level with her own. She grinned at him, and he laughed. Under the veneer of sophistication the old Penelope remained.

'Congratulations,' he said. 'Sorry I wasn't here for the wedding.'

'Oh—it wasn't a big one,' she said dismissingly. 'I don't go much on all that pomp stuff.' She did not add that Great-Aunt Hermione could not have stood the strain of a large gathering.

Philip, who had an eye for detail, noticed the beautiful diamond brooch which she wore pinned to the shoulder of her green velvet dress. It was a lovely piece, and valuable. He rummaged in his pocket and drew out a small parcel, which he thrust at her rather awkwardly.

'Bit late for a wedding present,' he said. 'Call it Christmas too. Not very thrilling, I'm afraid, nor useful, but I thought you'd have got all your cups and saucers and so on by this time.'

'Oh, Philip, how exciting!' She took the packet and opened the wrappings quickly. Inside there was a small cardboard box, and it contained a little ivory ship. It was a Chinese junk, complete with sails, slats and stays, but tiny, most intricately carved.

'Just a mascot, for luck,' he said. 'I saw it in a window.'

'It's lovely, Philip!' Her eyes were tremendous as she looked at him. 'Oh, thank you! I love it.'

He was glad she was pleased. She looked at it again, turning it over in her hand, and was going to speak when there was a noise outside in the hall. The other guests were arriving. Before they entered Vincent came in from the second door that led to the staircase, and there was just time for Penelope to introduce the two men before the room filled. She slipped the little ship into her bag, wrapped in its tissue paper.

Dr Torrington was a short man, like Philip, with sparse grey hair spread over his neat, round skull. He had merry eyes and was cheerful and rather hearty. His wife had the arresting colouring that Philip had inherited, clear pale skin and amber eyes, but her hair had faded now to pepper and salt. Her great grief was that she had no daughter to inherit her looks, but with her customary cynicism she reflected that, such being life, a daughter would have more probably repeated her husband's dark complexion and knock knees. While Dr Torrington lamented that his son had elected not to follow in his footsteps and study medicine, his wife looked forward with confidence, to the day when Philip would have his first West End success in the theatre.

Major Tompkins had almost no hair at all; his pate gleamed, and his forehead seemed enormous. His eyes, pale blue, shone beneath shaggy white brows whose luxuriance made amends for the dearth above, and he had a flowing white moustache which hid little pink lips like a child's. Penelope had never ceased to wonder why nature could arrange for so much hair on the face and none where it would look better. Major Tompkins had travelled a lot, chiefly with the Army, and had a fund of good, mostly repeatable, stories. Great-Aunt Hermione found him amusing, and because she was sure he was lonely, always invited him to Christmas dinner. Beside him tonight, fluttering rather, came Kitty Francis. She wore a blue dress made from handwoven material worked by herself on her own loom, and was hung about with jangling earrings and necklaces. She had grey hair cut in a fringe, and brushed down straight at the sides like a page in a fairy-tale. Great-Aunt Hermione sometimes suspected that she contrived her appearance especially to look as she thought everyone expected her to, knowing her artistic interests, and that really she would have been much more comfortable with a string of cultured pearls and a little black woollen frock off the peg of D. H. Evans or some similar store.

Everyone was drinking sherry: Vincent wandered about being host. He was good at it, his manners were impeccable. Penelope had often felt proud as he remembered to walk outside her on pavements; and now she was pleased as she saw him so naturally assuming the role of the son of the house.

Philip felt an absurd resentment as he watched Vincent with the decanter. It was ridiculous, the fellow was quite right, of course, it was his duty; but it had once been Philip who helped with such things. Vincent, the heavy decanter in his left hand, moved quietly round filling up the emptied glasses, and Philip's neck bristled with antagonism. He was glad when Cartwright announced dinner.

Queenie had surpassed herself. The turkey was moist, and tender as butter; and as in previous years Dr Torrington, with a smile at his hostess, rose automatically to carve it. He loved to do this job, and was not going to stand by and see it mishandled by Vincent. With neat, precise strokes he severed the sturdy legs, then sliced the plump breast and gave everyone pieces of both on their plates.

At first, during dinner, the talk was general, until Mrs Torrington asked Penelope about her Christmas presents. The brooch, glinting on her dress, was much admired.

'And Vincent gave her a doll, too, the most amazing thing,' said Great-Aunt Hermione. 'He saw it in a shop window in Chelsea. It looks exactly like Penelope.'

'Philip gave me something he saw in a shop window too,' said Penelope hurriedly. She did not want to talk about the doll. 'A wedding present. I haven't shown it to you, yet, darling,' she added, to Vincent. She opened her bag and drew out the little boat. It was handed round the table to be appraised, and then she put it down before her plate, where it remained for the rest of the meal.

But she was not to be allowed to forget the doll.

'A doll like you, eh?' said Major Tompkins. 'Ha, ha, mind you take care of it—don't want to go sticking any pins in it, do you?' He laughed, his moustaches vibrating with the movement.

'Voodoo dolls are made of wax,' said Vincent smoothly. 'Penelope's doll has a china face.'

'Oh, Fred, you don't believe in all that, do you?' said Kitty Francis. 'You mean making a waxen image of your deadliest foe and sticking pins in it to make it die?'

'A lot of nonsense,' said Vincent roundly.

'You think so, do you?' Philip looked consideringly at Vincent.

'No sensible person believes any of that,' said Vincent firmly. 'All the same, Fred, that was a funny business that happened out in Breya when we were there.'

'Oh, what? Have you got a creepy story for us?' said Kitty. 'I must say I do believe in ghosts. I once lived in a cottage where Coco—a poodle I had—refused to go into a particular room, and if you made him he howled and howled. Later I learned someone had hung themselves there, but I never saw anything.'

'But there must be nice ghosts too,' said Mrs Torrington. 'If you believe in them at all, that is.'

'Oh no,' cried Kitty. 'It's the souls of those who've died before their time, probably by violence, who can't find rest and haunt the earth.'

'Oh, how horrible,' shuddered Penelope. 'I wouldn't mind a gentle ghost, like Uncle Cedric. If he took to haunting us I wouldn't be afraid. But I don't like to think about poor, unhappy ghosts.'

'And don't you worry your pretty head about them, my sweet,' said Vincent from across the table. 'They don't exist. All the same, funny things do happen. What about the chief of Breya, Fred?' he repeated. 'Do you remember that business?'

'Do I not!' Major Tompkins looked round the assembled company. 'It was a funny affair. Of course, they said it was poison, but I don't see how it could have been.' He paused, gazing round. 'Do you want to hear it?' he asked. His eyes were alight with the treat he had in store for them; he laid down his knife and fork, ready to begin.

'Do tell us,' said Mrs Torrington, unnecessarily, for nothing would prevent him.

'Well, to understand this story you must first realize that when we arrived in West Africa we developed a policy of governing indirectly, through the established chiefs, but as education progressed and the desire for democracy grew, the chiefs we supported began to grow less powerful. Now at Breya, a town where I lived for some time, there was a particular chieftain who had a strange and mystical domination over all the people for miles around—a domination related, so it was said, to magic that was hereditary in his office.'

Here Major Tompkins paused to look about him at his audience.

'This chief was too proud to submit to the increasingly democratic development of the country,' he continued, 'so he declared that rights and votes talked of in distant cities were no concern of his. This made him very unpopular with the keen young politicians who stood for progressive western ways, and they threatened to arrest him. But time went on, and the chief stayed in power, and the people began to jeer at the politicians and say that their chief was a crafty old man, far cleverer than any of them. At last the politicians decided that something must be done to make the old chief toe the line, and they sent an English-trained lawyer, a big fat African called Willy Johnson, down to Breya with a charter for the chieftain to sign, greatly limiting his powers.

Word went out from Breya that the politicians were going to destroy the chief, and that his day was done.'

Major Tompkins stopped again. Equipped with a good story, he knew how to tell it to the best dramatic effect, and everyone was listening to him attentively. He took a breath and continued.

This was big news, and it buzzed in the markets and on the drums at night; it droned and thumped its way from Breya to the sea, and everyone who could do so travelled to the town to see what would happen when the chief surrendered to the politicians.

'So at last the day came. The chief sat in the outer compound of his palace, under the shaded arches of his throne room, visible to all; and the space in front of him was filled with hundreds of his people, waiting to watch what happened. The chief was splendid in his robes, with his councillors at his feet; and then in came the lawyer, Willy Johnson, and his supporters, all in dark suits with stiff collars, bringing the great charter.

'Willy Johnson read it slowly out to the chief, and when the people saw that he was going to accept it, and must therefore lose a lot of his power, a great clamour broke out among them. The chief had consented. His day was done, he had been beaten.

'But then the chief stood up. Silence fell as he held up his arms and beckoned Willy Johnson to stand in front of him. Before all the people he made a sign which meant that the lawyer was cursed. Then the crowd began to make a different noise, a murmuring. Johnson broke down and wept, and his friends hurried him out through the crowd to his car. They drove off as fast as they could back to the city, where they guarded him day and night, but in a week he was dead.'

There was complete silence when the Major ended his tale. He picked up his knife and fork again and went on with his turkey.

'Well!' Dr Torrington was the first to speak. 'Remarkable,' he said.

'Fear? He could have died of fright?' said Mrs Torrington.

'I believe it was witches,' said Kitty firmly. She shook her head till her earrings rattled. 'It must have been.'

'Well, they must exist, or evil spirits anyway,' said Great-Aunt Hermione, making her first contribution to the conversation. 'The Church has special services for exorcism, doesn't it?'

'I do believe that when you're in a terrible temper a sort of devil takes over,' said Penelope slowly. 'You do get possessed.'

Philip remembered her, scarlet-faced, aged eight, shouting at him because he was late when they were going out fishing. It turned out afterwards that she was afraid he had fallen off his bicycle and broken his neck, because she had heard Cartwright prophesy that fate for him if he rode it without hands on the main road. Her rage had been relief at his safety.

'It's not a devil, it's your subconscious,' he told her earnestly.

Penelope smiled. 'My subconscious must be very bad-tempered, then,' she said.

'Talking about ghosts, they are, and devils,' Cartwright told Queenie as he fetched the fruit and nuts.

'Whatever next?' She threw up her arms. 'And after that dinner, too, they'll all have nightmares.' She turned back to contemplate her goldfish, and tossed them a crumb of turkey meat to mark the day.

'Who's going to the Meet tomorrow?' Philip was determined to turn the conversation, which seemed to him morbid for Christmas night, and soon they began to discuss the prevalence of wire, the low funds of the hunt, and the rights and wrongs of blood sports.

'It's fun to watch, and fun to do, but anachronistic in our modern age,' said Philip.

'But you don't want to do away with all old things, all tradition, do you?' Kitty asked him. She was interested by Philip, whom she had not met before; she had arrived to live in Foxbourne St. Mary after his departure for America.

'No.' He looked at her attentively. 'I don't want to do away with hunting, really, but I'm sorry for the fox, sorrier for stags, and I don't want to do it again myself, though except for sailing I've known few excitements like it.'

'Killing,' said Major Tompkins, nodding his head. 'Killing, in hot blood, in war.'

'Well, Fred, I hope you've done no other kind,' remonstrated Kitty sharply.

Great-Aunt Hermione rose abruptly, and the other women also stood. 'Gentlemen,' she said, with a half smile, 'don't be long, we want your company, but leave your talk of death and ghosts and witches behind.'

After dinner they drank brandy and liqueurs, and they played silly paper games until Dr Torrington said they must go home. He had seen that Great-Aunt Hermione was beginning to look tired, and he knew the uncertain state of her heart. Overstrain now might mean several days in bed to recover, and although he was not in favour of restricting her activities so much as to deprive her of her few remaining pleasures, he thought it folly to court trouble.

The party began to break up. Kitty went happily off with the Major, and Dr and Mrs Torrington followed. Philip, who had forgotten all about his promise to go and see Queenie, suddenly thought of it and said he would go out to the kitchen for a word with her and then come on in his own car.

Soon they had all left the drawing-room. Vincent went out to the hall to see them off, and Great-Aunt Hermione turned to Penelope.

'I'm weary, pet, I'm going up,' she said. 'Pop in and say goodnight to me later.'

'I'll come up with you now,' said Penelope, looking at her anxiously.

'No—don't do that, I'm quite all right,' said the old lady. 'You wait for your Vincent, he'll want you to himself after the party. I'll just take my time.' She began to go slowly up the stairs. Penelope watched her till she had turned the bend and was out of sight, then she returned to the drawing-room. She was playing with her little Chinese ship, moving it up and down on the arm of the chair, when Vincent returned, and they were both walking upstairs together when there was a sudden dull thud from the big room that was Great-Aunt Hermione's, a thump like a heavy chair going over, and a cry.

Penelope gave a little shriek, dropped Vincent's arm and ran up the second flight of stairs. She burst into Great-Aunt Hermione's bedroom.

The old lady lay over the electric fire, where she had fallen, her right arm doubled under her, her gold dress already scorching.

Philip and Cartwright arrived from the other end of the landing by way of the back stairs. They had heard the noise from the kitchen, and came on the scene seconds after Vincent followed Penelope into the room. He stood blocking the doorway, and Philip thrust him aside, only vaguely hearing the astonished, 'What, already, Penelope?' above the girl's hysterical cries.

'Don't touch her,' Philip shouted, and pulled the electric plug out of the socket in the wall before he turned to the poor, twisted thing that had been Great-Hermione.

6

The body lay across the fire, the head lolling grotesquely, the left arm against the bars as though attempting to push it away. Philip and Cartwright turned it gently over. The face was contorted in a grimace.

'Dereham—take Penelope out of here—give her some brandy,' ordered Philip brusquely, putting himself between the body and the girl to screen the features from her.

Vincent had approached them and was staring at the scene; now he took Penelope's arm. She seemed frozen in horror, her crying ceased, and after one more half-mesmerised glimpse of the huddle on the floor she allowed herself to be led from the room.

The dead woman's hand held the tongs in a strong grip: they were wedged between the bars of the fireguard, against the metal. Gently Philip and Cartwright eased the fingers free.

'We'd better get my father,' said Philip, pushing a hand distractedly through his hair. Dishevelled, it stood up in an untidy thatch. 'She must have had a heart attack.'

'I never liked her using them tongs, but she would,' said Cartwright.

Philip stared down at the body. The right wrist had been doubled back, holding the tongs as she must have caught them when she fell, attempting to save herself.

'She couldn't have been going to curl her hair now, surely?' he said.

Cartwright shook his head.

'Oh, not this time of night—morning and evening, regular as clockwork, that's what she did,' he said. 'No, I expect she felt chilly and switched on for a bit of a warm—the radiators keep the room heated, but some nights she liked a bit extra. Queenie's found her asleep in her chair up here in front of the fire before now, very late. She always pops in last thing to see if everything's all right, and sometimes she wakes in the night worrying, and comes along. Mrs Vandyk missed the Colonel, you know. She was lonely.'

Cartwright was silent, and Philip looked miserably down at the staring eyes and twisted face. The indignity of death appalled him. 'Poor old lady,' he said.

'Don't take on, sir,' said Cartwright robustly. He guessed that Philip, in spite of his National Service, had not seen anything like this before. 'Best have a nip of brandy like Miss Penny. Will you ring the doctor or shall I?'

'Oh—I'll do it. Thanks, Cartwright. Will you go and tell Queenie what's happened, and then see if that fellow's looking after Penny? She's had an awful shock.'

'I'll go down now, Mr Philip,' said Cartwright.

Philip moved over to the white telephone that stood beside Great-Aunt Hermione's four-poster bed. His father would just have reached home now; he might catch him before he had put the car away and locked up. He dialled the number and while it rang stood looking down at the body where it still lay upon the floor. The urge to lift it and move it to the bed, and cover it decently, was strong in him, but obscurely something about the manner in which it had lain across the fire still puzzled him.

He turned away sharply when he heard his father's voice on the line.

'You're certain she's dead?' The incisive tones at the other end of the wire helped Philip to gather his scattered wits. It was odd to think of his father, relaxed and content such a short time before, suddenly alerted, standing beside his desk, head on one side, brain automatically clicking into action.

'No doubt about it at all, Father,' he replied. 'I should think she's had a heart attack, but she must have got a shock from the fire when she fell. She's a bit burnt about the arm.'

'Hm. Well, better leave her where she is till I get there,' said Dr Torrington. 'I'll be straight over, Philip.'

'Thanks,' Philip felt grateful. He put the receiver back; then he took the pink quilted eiderdown off the bed and gently draped it over Great-Aunt Hermione.

By three o'clock on the morning of Boxing Day Dr Torrington had finished his examination of the body. Great-Aunt Hermione had definitely not had a stroke; her death was due to heart failure and a severe electric shock received when she fell across the fire and grasped the tongs to save herself. It was possible that she had received the shock before her heart failed: she might have felt dizzy and lost her balance, falling on the fire and pushing the tongs into contact with the current as she did so. In whatever order the events had happened, both had combined to cause death.

Penelope's face was white as she listened while Dr Torrington told her this as gently as he could. She was trembling, but otherwise in command of herself: shock had numbed her.

'Come along, Penny love,' said Queenie. She had bustled in to make up the fire, and had brewed coffee for the doctor, as soon as Cartwright had told her about the tragedy. Now she ignored Vincent; had she not nursed Penny through measles and chicken-pox? It behoved her to do what she could to comfort her dear in this dreadful disaster. 'You must get some rest. There'll be things to do in the morning.'

'Yes, go along, Penny,' said Dr Torrington. 'My poor child, I know what this means to you, but you must try and get some sleep.'

'She couldn't have known anything, Penelope.' It was Vincent who spoke. 'It must have happened very quickly, isn't that right, doctor?'

'Oh—all over in a matter of a second or two,' said Dr Torrington briefly.

'She'd only just gone upstairs,' said Penelope. 'Only a few minutes before; then Vincent came in and we started to follow, and then the bump. I was to pop in and say "good-night", she'd said.' She shuddered.

'Don't you think about it, love,' advised Queenie. She put a stout arm round Penelope and glanced across at Vincent, consideringly. 'I'll just take her up and see she's cosy with a nice fresh hot-water bottle, sir,' she told him.

Vincent nodded. He turned with some authority to the other men. 'We'll have to notify the solicitor in the morning, and so on,' he said. 'And there will be an inquest, of course?'

'I'm afraid so. A mere formality but it must be,' said Dr Torrington. 'Try not to let Penelope know there must be a post-mortem—no point in upsetting her still more if we can avoid it.' He looked at the younger man. 'No point in worrying too much about any of that now,' he said briskly. 'I'll ring the coroner first thing—he may as well finish his night's sleep. If I were you I'd let Queenie see to Penelope, give them a quarter of an hour or so, and then take her up these tablets; that will make sure she'll get some sleep.'

Vincent nodded again and took the pills which the doctor gave him.

'Well, Philip—we can't do any more now,' said his father. 'Come along. We'll be over in the morning, Dereham.' He began to put on his thick brown coat which he had flung across a chair. Philip followed him out of the room, and Cartwright, with a shepherding motion, went behind them into the hall. Vincent, left alone, poured himself out some more brandy. He would certainly leave Queenie to deal with Penelope's tears. He looked consideringly down at the pills in his hand: then he threw them into the fire.

In the hall Philip hesitated. He looked at his father, and then said: 'I'll follow you, Father. I've forgotten something,' and turned back, leaving Cartwright to go out on to the gravel sweep with Dr Torrington and see him drive off in his big old Morris. Philip returned to the open doorway of the drawing-room, and stood unobserved for a moment watching Vincent. He saw the other man cross to the fire and bend over it for an instant. Then Philip moved quietly away and hurried upstairs. He went again into Great-Aunt Hermione's room, crossed to the bed and drew down the sheet which covered her. She looked less horrifying now, but his mouth tightened as he gazed at her for a minute. Then he covered her face again, and glanced across once more at the fire. After a few seconds' contemplation he picked it up, and the tongs, and put them both in the wardrobe among Great-Aunt Hermione's shoes. Then he went along the passage and tapped gently at Penelope's door.

Queenie opened it. Her round face was anxious and her brown eyes worried, but her expression lightened when she saw Philip.

'How is she?' he asked.

'Nearly asleep,' Queenie replied. Philip peered round the door and saw Penelope lying in bed, looking much as she had done a few years before after a fall from her pony and a minor concussion. The eiderdown was pulled up to her chin, and her face was as white as the pillow. Now, as then, she attempted to smile, and Philip experienced a pang that was part pity, part fear, and part some other unidentified emotion that he did not want to recognize.

'Hullo, Phil,' she said shakily.

He crossed to her side, and a hand came out from the bedclothes to grip his. He could think of nothing to say, while tears rolled once again down Penelope's face.

'Sorry,' she mumbled, finding her handkerchief and blowing her nose. Queenie, in the background, watching them, knew irrevocably that Philip, the trespasser, was by rights the man who ought to be here now, not Vincent, the interloper. She tiptoed out, leaving them, not daring to face her thoughts.

Philip found himself supporting Penny while she wept, a thin and shrinking creature, still a child, and murmuring useless words of comfort in her ear which from time to time he kissed. He rather hoped Vincent would walk in and find them so, except that Penny's attitude was, in fact, he knew, blameless. At last he left her.

'Ring up if you want anything, anything at all,' he said.

'Yes, Phil,' Penelope replied obediently. Her voice was high and light, and choked on a sob.

He glanced swiftly round the room. On the dressing-table he saw a small doll sitting, her skirts spread stiffly out, the back of the tiny dark head leaning against the mirror. At this distance, eighteen feet or more, the face was merely a blob, but the dark hair and the green dress were just like

Penelope's. Philip was puzzled and uneasy; but he could find no reason, apart from the tragedy that had befallen, for the fearful sense of forboding that now filled him, and it was not only jealousy, sharp and bitter, that he knew when he thought of Vincent. Philip withdrew, and as he disappeared down the back staircase Penelope's husband reached the landing by way of the front.

7

The inquest was soon over. Penelope, because she had found the body, was compelled to give evidence, but her part in the proceedings was brief, and she returned to sit beside Queenie on a bench in the bleak, hastily-opened school building. Queenie, her coat with the beaver collar marked now with a sombre black band round the sleeve, took the girl's cold hand and patted it. Vincent, on Penelope's other side, was listening intently to what was being said in the makeshift coroner's court.

Dr Torrington gave evidence that Great-Aunt Hermione had suffered for some years from a chronic condition of degeneration of the heart, slowly worsening but not surprising in someone of her age. He had expected her to decline more rapidly during the coming year, and though her death had been sudden, with a heart as uncertain as hers such a thing could not be a complete surprise.

A verdict of death due to natural causes was recorded, the coroner adding that the deceased had suffered a severe electrical shock which had contributed, and warning the assembled company not to take risks with electrical appliances.

After the funeral Penelope and Vincent returned to London. She was exhausted by nights with little or no sleep, and stunned by the suddenness of shock and the grief of bereavement. Vincent was very patient. He told

Queenie, when she hesitatingly suggested that Penelope might like to remain at Greyfriars for a little while to recover, that he thought she would be better away from the scene where the unhappy business had happened, with all its memories, and that he would take great care of her. Later, when she was ready, they would return and decide what to do about the house, for as Queenie and Cartwright must know, lawyers moved slowly and the will would take some time to prove.

In spite of their uneasiness, they were powerless in face of his obvious practical grasp of the situation; he had dealt with *The Times* and *The Daily Telegraph*, the undertaker and Mr Simpson the solicitor. He had forgotten nothing, and his assumption of authority commanded their respectful obedience.

'I'll come up straight away if you need me,' Queenie told Penelope as she packed for her. She wrapped up the china doll carefully and stowed it between two of her soft woollen jerseys. 'Just ring up and I'll get on the very next train.'

'Thank you, Queenie.' Penelope was grateful, but she knew she must manage. Now she must grow up.

Back in Kensington she tried desperately hard to pull herself together. She was still appalled by the suddenness with which tragedy could strike, and she was scarcely able to think past the fact of Great-Aunt Hermione talking to her at one minute and lying dead within five more.

'But sweetheart, look how much better that was for her than a lingering illness,' said Vincent one evening a week later. They were sitting facing one another on either side of the electric fire in their little sitting-room. Penelope's thin fingers played restlessly with the ends of a silk scarf tied round her neck. She had worn her black coat for the funeral, but was now dressed in a pale beige woollen dress with a brown printed square at her throat. She knew that Great-Aunt Hermione would have held up her hands in dismayed horror if she had gone into mourning. 'You don't want to embarrass your friends,' she had said when Uncle Cedric had died. 'Just keep your sadness inside.'

Vincent was watching her, his eyes narrowed, very light blue in the reflection of the standard lamp over his head.

'Yes, I know—but I'd been telling her how dangerous that fire was,' said Penelope wretchedly.

'But my dear, it wasn't anything to do with the fire, it was heart failure,' said Vincent patiently. 'After all, everyone has to die sometime, we can't avoid it, and she was lucky. She knew nothing.'

'Oh, I know—but I always thought that a person was meant to die at a special time,' said Penelope. 'I can't believe it was intended that she should die on Christmas night. I keep wondering if the fire hadn't been there whether she might have got better.'

'Do you think it was meant that your own mother should die when you were a baby?' asked Vincent.

'No—yes—I don't know,' said Penelope. 'There must have been a reason. Nowadays she wouldn't have, I suppose, doctors are cleverer. '

Vincent stared at her.

'But didn't you know?' he asked, and then added, 'No, of course not, no one would tell you.'

She was frightened. He was looking at her strangely. 'Tell me what? What is it, Vincent?' Penelope sat up straight in her chair, both hands grasping its arms.

'No—no—it's nothing.' Vincent took out his gold cigarette case and selected a cigarette. He tapped it on the back of the case; thump, thump, the tiny sound seemed to batter on Penelope's ear-drums. She bit her lip.

'There is something. Please, Vincent. What do you know about my mother?' she asked.

Vincent lighted his cigarette before replying. She could have screamed with impatience, waiting while he inhaled deeply and then blew out columns of smoke down his nostrils.

'Well,' he said at last, reflectively, 'I suppose you'll have to know one day.' He paused, looking down at his cigarette. Then he looked at her, seeming to make up his mind. 'Your mother committed suicide,' he said.

'Oh no!' Penelope stared at him, eyes huge in her white face. She shrank back into her big chair. 'Oh no,' she said again. 'She couldn't have.'

'She did. She took sleeping pills,' said Vincent.

'But—but she died after I was born,' Penelope said. 'Aunt Hermione told me.'

'It was quite soon after you were born,' Vincent replied. 'Your father had been killed when his ship was torpedoed; she was temporarily out of her mind.'

'But Aunt Hermione always said —' Penelope's head swam. Great-Aunt Hermione had made it a pathetic, moving tale: the handsome young sailor killed in the war, and his grieving widow dead after Penelope's birth, both together in Heaven, she had been told as a child; and the elderly pair, Great-Aunt Hermione and Great-Uncle Cedric, given new life by the child that they cherished. Where was this pretty story now?

'Of course, you had to be told something,' Vincent was saying. 'A child couldn't be told the truth.'

'No. No, I suppose not,' said Penelope. 'But when I grew up?'

'But are you grown up yet?' asked Vincent. 'Isn't that why you won't face up to what I've been telling you?'

Penelope closed her eyes. She was nearly nineteen. She was a married woman. This must be true. No one would invent such a tale, and least of all Vincent, whom she trusted absolutely, did she not?

'I believe you,' she said at last, opening her eyes.

'And you must try, my dear, to be calm,' said Vincent. 'Of course, your mother had been through a very unhappy time, but these things can run in families, tendencies to do the same things, and so on.'

'But you don't mean I'd do such a thing?' Penelope exclaimed in horror. 'Of course I wouldn't! Why, I've everything to live for!'

'Of course you have, my sweet,' said Vincent, rising. He stubbed out his cigarette very slowly. Vincent did everything in a leisurely way. Then he crossed over to her chair. 'Dear child, don't be unhappy,' he said. Over the top of his shoulder as he loomed above her the doll, unblinking, stared down in mockery from the mantelpiece.

That night Vincent was especially thoughtful and solicitous. He decided that she must go early to bed, and brought her supper on a tray, preparing it all himself—soup, and poached eggs on toast. When she had laboriously swallowed it he returned with hot milk and two aspirins.

'You mustn't get into the way of taking pills,' he told her. 'But you're upset tonight. Take them and get some sleep.'

He left the tablets beside her. Penelope stared at them. Her mother must have had a full bottle. Aspirins, were they? Or pheno-barbitone, like Aunt Hermione's little white pills? Her knowledge of such things was small. Her mother must have emptied the bottle. Did she swallow them all one by one, with sips of water, or dissolve them in something hot? What did they taste like? Surely a quantity of tablets dissolved would be like porridge? She shuddered. Her mother had been very young, only twenty-two, not much older than she was now. Her father and she had only had a few weeks together before he went off to sea and was killed. Death—the one inescapable fact. You could run away from everything else but not from death. It waited for everyone, like a tiger, lying in ambush for some, ready to spring suddenly, and creeping up slowly on others, with stealth, reluctant to end the by-play of cat with mouse. Penelope closed her eyes, but panic hit her. She sat up in bed. The aspirins stared at her from the table where Vincent had laid them. A thick skin had formed on the cooling milk. She sipped it: it was lukewarm and nauseating. There would be more aspirins in the bottle: it lived on the bathroom shelf, she had only to fetch it. There were a hundred in it at least, that should be plenty.

Aghast, Penelope suddenly realized the drift of her thoughts. She got out of bed and picked up the two tablets. Then she went over to the window and opened it, flinging them out into the street with all her force.

Vincent entered then and found her leaning against the window staring out, the chill wind blowing the net curtain against her thin figure in the white silk nightdress.

'Penelope, my dear,' he said, his voice carefully lowered. 'What are you doing? You'll catch cold. Into bed now.' He propelled her gently back and tucked her in. 'No more running about,' he admonished her. 'Why, you've let your milk get cold. I'll heat it up.' He carried it away. Penelope could not tell him she did not want it when he was being so kind, and when he returned she had not the strength of will to send it after the aspirins on to the pavement below.

Vincent watched her drink it, and then went away with the empty glass and washed it up. When he returned he carried the doll.

'Look, you left her behind on the mantelpiece,' he said, putting her down on the pillow beside Penelope.

The doll's tiny body was hard. Penelope put two fingers round its waist, gripping it.

Vincent said: 'You're very tired, dear. I'll sleep in the other room tonight, then you'll be undisturbed.'

She did not want to be alone, but she did not want Vincent: she was lost and terrified, unable to bear her thoughts.

Very quietly he was moving about the room picking up his possessions—pyjamas, dressing-gown, brushes. Then he tiptoed out. She heard the door softly close, and then the final sound of the little spare bedroom's door across the landing. She sat up, wanting to call him back, but she could not.

Under her hand the body of the doll was very small. She picked it up, peering at it in the darkness which was broken by the reflection of light from the street outside. Then she flung the doll across the room. The noise it made, splintering into fragments against the skirting, seemed deafening to Penelope. She waited, but there was no sound except the loud, irregular thump of her heart.

Trembling, she pulled the bedclothes up over her head and lay beneath them, rigid. She remained like that for hours, until near dawn nature at last gave her the brief, exhausted respite of oblivion.

8

Vincent was good about the breakage of the doll. Penelope, half-hysterical about how she was to explain, scooped up all the bits as soon as she awoke and put them carefully in a little heap on the window sill.

'I knocked her over. I'm so sorry,' she said apologetically.

'My dear, don't worry,' said Vincent. 'It was an accident. You're overwrought, and that makes you clumsy. Besides, she's your doll, not mine.' He picked up some of the pieces. The head was held together by the wig, but the face was shattered.

'She's too badly broken to mend,' Penelope hazarded.

'I'm afraid so.' Vincent frowned over the fragments. 'What a pity. Still, we'll see.' He went out of the room and she heard his footsteps on the stairs. Soon he returned carrying a large envelope, and he carefully put all the wreckage inside. Then he kissed her on the side of her head and went off to work.

Penelope no longer got her housework done in a couple of hours. She dragged round with the Hoover and a duster, her body aching with weariness and her head thumping. When the telephone rang the sound of the bell made her jump and she knocked a china shepherdess off the mantelpiece. Another breakage.

'Hullo? Penny?' it was a man's voice on the line, and she did not recognize it.

'It's Philip. I say, I'm in town for the day, how about lunching with me?'

'Oh!' Penelope could not answer at first. Her mind took a few seconds to adjust from the limbo of abstract misery to the new situation. 'Thank you,' she temporized.

'Well, good.' Philip seemed to think it was settled. 'I'll pick you up,' he told her. 'Half-past twelve.'

'All right.'

She hung up the receiver. It was twelve o'clock now, and there was immediately the necessity for putting on clothes suitable for going out to lunch. The mechanical task of doing this occupied her full concentration. She wondered vaguely if Vincent would mind her lunching with Philip: he knew they were childhood friends, so surely he would not object. For a moment she thought of ringing him up to make sure, and went so far as to consult the directory for the telephone number of Automobile Kings, Ltd., but he had asked her never to telephone unless it was a real emergency. He was often in conference, he said, and unnecessary interruptions were to be deplored, much as he would like to chat with her during the day if he had time to waste. The sound of Philip ringing the front-door bell brought her speculations to an abrupt halt and she hastened to let him in.

'I say, how jolly nice,' he exclaimed, entering the tiny hall, determined to be brisk.

'Isn't it?' She was pleased. 'Come and see the rest.'

Philip shot a shrewd glance at her as she led the way upstairs. Her face when she opened the door had horrified him, white, and with huge circles round her dark eyes. She was grieving still, but what else was wrong? He feared to know. He followed her round the little house, enthusing over what he saw in a way that gratified her. The kitchen was the epitome of modernity.

'Can you cook, Penny?' he asked.

'Oh yes,' she replied. 'Queenie taught me, I always used to love helping her.'

'Well, if you can cook like Queenie, Dereham's a lucky fellow,' said Philip, about to add, 'No wonder he looks so sleek,' but tactfully he refrained.

'Aunt Hermione gave us the house. She paid for it all as a wedding present,' said Penelope. Her lip quivered. 'She'd never been to stay,' she added.

Philip looked at her. Her head was lowered, turned away from him. He took her elbow and moved her round to face him.

'Penny,' he said commandingly.

She met his gaze. He saw again the evidence of exhaustion on her face.

'You're still very upset,' he told her. She nodded. A tear suddenly ran down her cheek.

'Poor old Penny, so'm I,' he said gruffly. The next minute she was weeping into his grey tweed shoulder, the first real tears she had shed since those on Christmas night. Philip again put an arm round her, found a clean handkerchief for her and held her, patting her gently at intervals and murmuring soothingly. He felt very sad himself.

'She wouldn't want us to be miserable, you know,' he said after a time.

'I know. It was just all so horrible and quick,' said Penelope. She blew her nose vigorously and wiped her eyes.

'Better than being bedridden for months,' said Philip.

'Yes. But the time wasn't right, somehow,' said Penelope.

' "To everything a season", you mean?' Philip quoted.

Gratefully she answered. 'Yes. "A time to be born, and a time to die." '

' "A time to mourn"?' Philip looked at her.

'Oh, how well you understand,' she said warmly. Philip was taken aback. Surely that Dereham fellow did? No, of course he didn't.

'Penelope, are you all right?' he asked very seriously. 'I mean—Vincent?' Somehow he uttered the outrageous name.

'Oh yes. He's very good to me,' she answered at once, not seeming to resent the enquiry as he feared she might, but she turned away, avoiding his eye.

'Well then, come along. Lunch.' Philip gave her a little shake. 'Go and wash your face and put on your prettiest hat, and we'll be off.'

He went into the sitting-room to wait for her, and she hurried upstairs. He heard her moving about above. Poor darling Penny, she was such a kid, and all alone now. Dereham, with the best will in the world, couldn't be expected to understand what the loss of Great-Aunt Hermione meant to her, and Philip doubted if he had that will. He wandered round the small room, looking with the inquisitive eye of the writer at its contents—the miscellany of objects, including the ivory ship he had given Penelope, on the mantelpiece; out of the window at the street where his car waited below; and at the bookshelf where a few novels and the works of Shakespeare and Wordsworth were displayed. Penelope, when last he knew her, had been a devotee of Baroness Orczy and D. K. Broster, and not far past the admirable works of Miss Lorna Hill and Mr Arthur Ransome. He lifted out the Wordsworth. 'Penelope Burton, St. Maud's School. Prize for Endeavour, 1955,' he read on the fly-leaf. He put the book back on the shelf. Penelope had always been a trier. He remembered her practising for a gymkhana, furious with impotent rage, straddled on the back of Tootles, her first pony, frantically trying to goad the unwilling animal down a line of bending poles arranged in the paddock at Greyfriars, while Cartwright yelled encouragement. On the day, fat Tootles had been third. She would try at this marriage of hers. Philip frowned. He knew himself prejudiced; that was of course why he could not accept it at its face value; there was no other valid reason.

He wandered across to a small mahogany desk that stood in a corner. A wilting cyclamen in a china pot was on the top of it: Philip grinned. Poor Penny, she evidently hadn't a hand for cyclamen. He felt the corm: it was saturated.

Suddenly, on impulse, he opened a drawer of the desk. Inside were a few envelopes, one of them bulky. He swiftly withdrew it and peered inside. It contained the broken fragments of a small doll. The head was missing, just the shattered torso and the limbs remained. Philip put it quickly back and closed the drawer, feeling very much ashamed of himself but at the same time puzzled.

When Penelope appeared a few moments later he was standing by the bookshelf busy reading *The Happy Warrior*.

They drove off noisily in the M.G. The hood was up in deference to Penelope; when alone, Philip drove through almost every kind of weather unprotected. He took her to a small restaurant in Soho and they had an excellent meal. Over it, he told her that he was in London to discuss the publication of his first book which had just been accepted. It was a novel about life on a newspaper in a small American town, powerful but not sordid, he told her, and he had worked at it during all his spare time in the last years. She was delighted with his success, and he went on to tell her about the plays he had written and would write.

At the end of an hour she discovered she had eaten a complete meal with enjoyment for the first time since Great-Aunt Hermione died.

'What would you like to do now?' Philip asked. 'Got a lot of chores?'

She shook her head.

'Let's go to the flicks, then,' said Philip.

'Oh, Philip, should we?' Penelope was rather startled. 'Aunt Hermione —' she stopped.

'"A time to laugh",' he told her. 'It will do you good.' During lunch he had noticed the shaking of her hands and the way she jumped when, with a clatter, someone in the kitchen dropped a dish.

'Have you seen my father lately?' he enquired as they drove off in search of somewhere to park near the cinema.

'Not since the funeral,' she said. 'We came straight back to London.'

'You'll be going down to see to things at Greyfriars?'

'I suppose so.' She sighed. 'I haven't thought about it. Vincent and the solicitor are seeing to everything.'

'Well, go over and see him when you do go down,' Philip said lightly. 'Father and Mother would both love to see you.'

'I will if I can,' she promised. She suddenly longed to tell Philip of the horrifying revelation Vincent had made to her about her own mother; but she could not. It was too terrible, and it meant facing the fact that Great-Aunt Hermione had embroidered the truth until it became fantasy. Philip glanced sideways at her. She was staring straight ahead into the traffic, tense in her seat. He wondered what sort of a driver Dereham was: one who cut in and braked sharply, he guessed, slowing down.

In the cinema fatigue and reaction combined to overwhelm Penelope. She struggled politely to keep her eyes open as the airless warmth rose to engulf her, but her attention would not remain on the screen, and exhaustion triumphed. Startled at seeing her sway, Philip looked at her in the darkness. Soon she gave up struggling, leaned against his shoulder and slept.

She was back in the little house again long before Vincent returned from Automobile Kings, Ltd. Philip had promised to ring her up the next time he was in London, and had airily waved aside her apologies at having slept throughout the film.

'Do you good, old dear,' he said cheerfully. 'Now don't go on fretting, will you? Or if you feel like it, have a good cry and get it off your chest.'

She nodded.

'Call me in if you like,' he added casually. 'I've usually got a clean hanky somewhere around.' He was unable to picture her cosily weeping on Vincent's wide shoulder, and felt that a stiff upper lip was required in that presence. He drove off, not at all reassured, with a good deal of noise from the exhaust of his car.

Penelope had intended to tell Vincent the details of how she had spent her day, but he defeated her. He came into the house, earlier than usual, and took off his coat in the hall. Then he handed her a small parcel.

'Look, sweetheart. I know you'll be pleased,' he said.

Slowly, with a sinking heart, she untied the string and removed the brown paper wrapping. Beneath was a shiny white box. Inside, eyes closed, dark hair neatly in place round the small pointed face, was a china doll in a green velvet dress.

9

The fact that she was to inherit a small fortune had not penetrated far into Penelope's head. Mr Simpson the solicitor, the bank, and Vincent between them seemed to be dealing with all that must be done, and it was with a shock that she remembered one day her aunt's intention to leave Philip part of her estate.

Great-Uncle Cedric had tied up his money so that it was willed directly to Penelope, but Great-Aunt Hermione had money of her own; this must be the amount she had meant to bequeath to her godson. All entail ceased with Penelope; trusts had proved lately to defeat the object of their creation, and the money was hers now unreservedly.

She mentioned the subject of Philip to Vincent.

'Oh yes, the old lady was talking about that the night she died, wasn't she?' he remembered at once.

'It seems very bad luck that he didn't get his share,' said Penelope. 'I shall give it to him.'

Vincent's eyes hardened. 'He won't accept it,' he told her. 'And the bank and Mr Simpson won't let you mess about with it till you're of age. Anyway probate won't be granted for some time.'

All this was patently true. Some control was imposed till she reached her majority. Doubtless also Philip would refuse to sign things; Penelope knew you could not do much without signatures.

'Perhaps I could back one of his plays,' she thought aloud. 'Yes, that's what I'll do.' She was sure she could convince Mr Simpson that this would be a wise move and consistent with Great-Aunt Hermione's plans. This decided, she put away the thought for the present. Philip, with his book coming out, his fast M.G. and his nice grey suit was obviously in funds for the moment. If things grew desperate and penury threatened him she would doubtless hear and could take action.

'You can't do much till the will is proved,' said Vincent.

Penelope knew that the bank was now eager to cash limitless cheques for her: but Vincent was right about the capital. He himself spent much time perorating at the iniquity of death duties and bewailing that Great-Uncle Cedric had not taken the prudent step of making his money over to Penelope five years before his own death. She writhed. She was grateful for what she would have and could not bear to think in those terms. It would be nice to be rich, but as she had never been really poor the full glory of complete financial security was outside her comprehension. She thought vaguely in terms of a proper fur coat, squirrel, perhaps, with wide cuffs; and more daringly of a Bentley for Vincent. He would like that.

'Now what are your plans for tomorrow?'

It was rare for Vincent to question her, but usually if she was going out she volunteered the information without being asked. Now she reminded him that she had a dentist's appointment in the morning and was then going to lunch with a married school friend in Chelsea.

'If course, I'd forgotten,' said Vincent. 'It will be nice for you. Take care, won't you?'

She was touched. 'Oh yes,' she said at once, though nice was not how she would have described her morning engagement.

The next day she hurried to tidy the house. Her appointment with Mr Gumming was for half-past eleven, and she took a bus to the West End, where he had his consulting rooms.

Mr Gumming soon filled up the painful small hole which had caused her to seek his assistance. He was a plump middle-aged man to whom she had been taken by Great-Aunt Hermione from the time that she was seven years old, pleasant and kind, not very talkative. He expressed sorrow about Great-Aunt Hermione, then fell to picking and scraping away at her teeth, uttering little sounds of concern now and then which alarmed her but proved to be needless.

'Rinse now, please,' he said at last, as if regretting that there was not more work for him to do.

Penelope rinsed, and then hopped down quickly from his high seat before he could change his mind and find further trouble. Soon she was out in the street walking away to catch another bus out to Chelsea. She had slept better the last few nights, since Philip had taken her out, and had summoned up the energy to invite herself over to see Betty with the idea that if she made more effort to snap out of her woe, her misery might lessen.

It had been raining again, and the pavements were greasy. London was full of bargain hunters come up for the January sales, and the streets were crowded with scurrying shoppers. Penelope hurried along to the bus stop. There was a small queue of people waiting, and when the bus arrived she was one of the last to mount. She stepped forward, and as she put one foot on the platform the other heel seemed to collapse under her: she stumbled backwards and fell over into the road. A woman behind her stooped forward to help her up.

'Oh, poor thing, you caught your foot,' she exclaimed. 'Are you hurt?' Kindly hands seized her by the arm.

Penelope's face flamed with mortification as she hastily picked herself up.

I'm quite all right, really,' she said quickly. 'Thank you so much.' The woman, quite young, with a long umbrella tucked under her arm, still held her elbow.

'You must be shaken,' she insisted. 'Oh look, mud on your coat.'

'Oh dear, so there is.' Penelope looked down. 'Really, I'm quite all right, though, thank you,' she added. Her one idea was to escape from her conspicuous position and leap on to the bus.

'If you are all right, miss?' The conductor, thinking of his schedule, bent down from the platform and held out his hand. Penelope accepted it and stepped, this time very carefully, on board. She went on into the bus and took a vacant seat right in front, filled with humiliation. Her shins ached and she had torn both her stockings; her right thigh felt bruised: she would be black and blue, and her coat was well spattered with mud as the kindly onlooker had pointed out. How incredibly stupid and clumsy she was!

The woman who had helped her took the seat behind, leaned forward, and said earnestly, 'Are you really all right?'

'Oh yes.' Penelope felt she would scream if the creature did not leave her alone, but she tried to seem grateful. She turned, with an attempt at a polite smile, and the woman's umbrella handle, made in the shape of a bird's head, poked into her shoulder. Penelope noticed a long scratch on the beak.

At Knightsbridge the woman got off, and Penelope settled back as they went along Sloane Street and then the King's Road. Her bruises throbbed. She looked out of the window trying not to think of them. In sympathy, the lately-drilled tooth also began to ache. She gazed steadily at the passing shops. Down one of these side streets Vincent had found the china doll. She wondered idly where the shop was. It was very good of him to get it replaced after she had broken it. She sighed. The new one had a tiny flaw on one leg, below the knee. Looking down, twisting in her seat, she saw the discolouration already beginning to show on her own, and when she touched it the mound of swelling could plainly be felt. Her heart raced uncomfortably; how odd that she had hurt herself just where the doll had been marked.

The next stop was hers. She got up and went carefully down the bus.

'Mind how you go, miss,' said the conductor, handing her out. She smiled absently at him and stepped off the kerb behind the bus almost into the oncoming traffic. Someone grabbed her arm and she backed hastily on to the pavement again. What a fool she was! She walked briskly along on the same side of the road for a while, before attempting to cross it again, until ahead she saw a zebra crossing.

A few minutes later she was walking down the quiet road where Betty lived. A row of tall houses ran down one side of it, and gardens behind sooty black railings were on the other. No one was in sight. Suddenly a big black Humber came down the road behind her, jammed on its brakes, skidded, and swerved on to the pavement, missing her by inches; then it roared on up the quiet street with tremendous acceleration and vanished out of sight round the corner. Penelope, trembling, clutched the railings above the area of the house outside which it had happened. She felt sick, and her knees shook. Presently she pulled herself together enough to walk the rest of the way to Betty's door.

Very soon she was feeling better. Betty, appalled at her ashen face and state of dishevellment, bathed her bruises, lent her another pair of stockings, and sat her down with a large gin and tonic. She was a plump, fair girl, a little older than Penelope, married to an architect, and she had a small son aged two and a daughter of three months old.

'But how perfectly ghastly, my dear! Did you take the idiot's number?' Betty was horrified by Penelope's tale of adventure. While she listened, she was busy mixing up her son's meal, turning it into a veritable dog's dinner in a bowl painted with the adventures of Jemima Puddleduck.

'No—it was all too quick—I didn't think of it till he'd gone out of sight. Besides, he didn't hit me. He skidded, there was an awful screech and I jumped out of the way.' She shuddered. 'There must have been a dog in the road, or something.'

'You poor old thing,' said Betty. 'Come on, Steve.' She heaved her son up into his high chair and gave him a pair of spoons, one for each hand. 'Eat up,' she begged, setting his plate in front of him.

The little boy needed no urging. Fair, silken head waving from side to side, he prodded the mixture speculatively. Then he began conveying it up to his mouth very rapidly, spilling a good deal down his bib and the front of the chair.

Penelope found herself presently sitting in front of the nursery fire giving the baby its bottle. She and Betty had eaten their own lunch perched on stools in the kitchen, shepherd's pie, and stewed rhubarb out of a tin, and then hurried to answer the wails and small waving fists from the pram in the postage-stamp garden behind the house.

'Peace after this,' Betty had promised, putting Stephen to bed for his sleep. Now, while Penelope dealt with the baby, Betty was ironing, and at the same time giving her a stern lecture on not being morbid, the need for proper sleep, and looking both ways before crossing the road.

It was warm in the nursery, with the gas fire brightly burning and the pile of ironed baby clothes hanging round it on the brass-railed fireguard. The baby, held very carefully in the crook of Penelope's inexperienced arm, was light and soft, and so alive, her little legs kicking enthusiastically and her hands patting the bottle with deep appreciation as she feasted. Her small head was rather bald, covered with the merest fluff of soft brown. Betty's words washed vaguely over Penelope as she concentrated on the job in hand.

Her afternoon was diverting, if not very restful, and she had no more adventures on the way home that evening.

She told Vincent that she had stumbled getting on the bus and bruised her shin. The mark, as large as a hen's egg, was clearly visible now under her stocking. Later she looked at the doll once again. As she had thought, the small flaw was on the left leg, like her bruise, right in the middle of the shin. Slowly she turned the doll round. The little green dress was fastened with small hooks at the back. Penelope began to undo it and then took it off; beneath, petticoat and tiny pants were beautifully made, hand sewn and finished with threadlike wisps of white lace, perfect in every detail. Under the left breast of the doll there was another flaw, the tiniest crack, nearly invisible, across the body. Very slowly Penelope began to put the clothes back again. The dress had a very faint smear on the velvet, a shine on the material as if it had brushed against something wet. She frowned, unable to remember spilling anything near it or splashing it.

That night she dreamed that the doll had pushed her off a bus under the wheels of a big black car.

10

Philip was walking along Piccadilly a week later. He had come to London to try and interest an editor in a series of articles he proposed to write. The interview had gone well, culminating in an invitation to lunch, so that he had reason to feel cheerful as he strode along; but though satisfied about this, he was not happy. He could not put the thought of Penelope out of his mind for long. He passed Burlington House, reading the notices of the exhibition inside as he went; then he turned up Bond Street. At Charbonnel and Walker's he was reminded of Penelope's past fondness for their wares, so he entered the shop and bought her a box of chocolate creams. When he emerged it was three o'clock and the February sky was grey. London was dark and gloomy. Philip had left his car in Hanover Square, and he turned towards it, still thinking of Penelope and with the parcel swinging from a finger. As he walked he looked idly at the windows of the shops and the faces of the passing people, for it was a habit of his to notice his surroundings. A row of dolls standing among some china ornaments in a small shop caught his eye. There was something familiar about them: they were about ten inches tall, china, with pale pointed faces. Philip stopped and stared. He had seen one like that before and it did not take him long to remember where.

He thought back to the dinner party on Christmas night and the conversation about Vincent giving Penelope one that he had seen in the King's Road. He remembered the little creature in green velvet that he had seen on her dressing-table later, after Great-Aunt Hermione had died. He had not seen it at very close quarters, it was true, but unless he was mistaken it was very like these in the window. There was a distinct resemblance between the dark-haired ones and Penelope; they were dressed in different peasant costumes, and some were fair-haired, all with long plaits. None was in modern dress.

On impulse, Philip went into the shop.

A blonde girl, very tall, wearing a lot of green eye-shadow which alarmed Philip, uncoiled herself from a chair in the corner and swam enquiringly over the carpet towards him. He smiled nervously; she was some inches taller than he. He cleared his throat and said: 'Er—I was—I noticed those dolls. Interesting. How much are they?'

'Five guineas each, sir,' she said. 'They're made in Germany and specially imported. All the costumes are authentic national dress, and we also have them in historical dress but at the moment we're out of stock of those. We'll be having more in, of course.'

'Charming,' said Philip in a Blimp-ish voice, inspecting them from the back; they were arranged on a glass shelf looking out of the window towards the passers-by. 'Do you sell many? Who buys them—collectors?'

'Yes, chiefly. We don't sell a lot of them, but at Christmas people buy them as presents, that's why we're down on the historical ones,' the girl said.

'Do you ever have modern ones?'

'Oh no, they're all either these or the old-fashioned ones,' she replied.

'What sort of people collect them?' asked Philip.

'Oh, various. Actresses, and society women, and so on. We had a man in the other day to replace one he'd bought for his small daughter—she'd broken it. Fancy spending all that on a child,' said the girl, forgetting her sophistication briefly.

Philip remembered the fragments he had seen in Vincent's desk drawer.

'Oh—what bad luck,' he said vaguely. 'The child breaking it, I mean.'

'Yes. I felt rather sorry for the father—he was a widower, he said. He bought the first one quite a while before Christmas. The second one was only a few days ago. I told him I was sure the kid would prefer one of those washable ones with hair you can perm, but he would insist on this sort.'

'Oh.' Philip picked up one of the dolls, a Dutch girl in a blue dress, and idly turned it over. Under the full skirts he saw wisps of white silk and lace.

The girl said: 'All the clothes are made by hand, and they all unfasten.'

Philip said abruptly: 'I'll have this one. I know a girl who might like it.' He hoped he had five guineas. He took out his wallet and counted: just enough. He watched the girl as she wrapped the doll up carefully in tissue paper and put it in a shiny white cardboard box: 'Young, was he, the widower with the daughter?'

'Oh yes—about thirty-five,' said the girl at once. 'Tall, you know. Fair—rather good-looking. Army, I'd say, with a small moustache.

'Oh,' Philip nodded.

'Harrow tie,' she added, glancing at Philip's rather worn Wykhamist one, which he had put on to impress the editor. 'I usually look.' Her customers were not often as pleasant as Philip, and she was bored with the weeks of slack business after Christmas. She finished tying up the parcel neatly, and gave it to him. He tucked it under his arm. Then he looked at the other one, the square box of chocolates, and suddenly handed it over the counter.

'The doll's a replacement for these,' he said. 'You have them, please.'

'Oh!' She was surprised. 'Thank you,' she said, in a half-protesting tone.

'Two presents for one girl are one too many,' said Philip. 'I'd like you to have them.'

She repeated: 'Thank you again,' and picked up the parcel. She looked after Philip in some astonishment as he left the shop without another word.

He hurried away. The girl would remember him, that was certain. In the car he unwrapped the doll and inspected it closely. If it was Vincent who had posed as a widower and bought the two dolls Penelope would have another in the house, replacing the one that lay in pieces in the drawer. He started his engine and edged out into the traffic in the direction of Kensington, fuming with impatience when he was delayed by the lights and by the blocks of cars and buses that he met, but at last he entered the quiet road which ran down to the mews, and turned the corner by the house with the shrivelled tree that drooped over the shabby railings. He had noticed this tree on his previous visit to Penelope, and glanced cursorily at it again now as he changed gear. It looked dead. A few dry husks clung to the branches here and there. He roared in low gear past Chez Miriam down the quiet little street to Penelope's door and came to a stop, all standing.

She took some time to let him in.

'Oh—Philip.' She looked startled, and half turned round as if someone was behind her. Her hair was untidy and her eyes large in a face that was chalk-white.

'Penny, you aren't well,' said Philip, striding firmly into the hall.

'I—no, I haven't been very well for a few days,' she admitted. 'I'm better now. I'm afraid the house is in an awful muddle, Philip, I haven't been bothering about it, but come in.'

'I'm in,' he said.

She dithered in front of him, and he looked at her closely. The unnamed fear that filled him rose up at her haggard appearance and made it hard for him to think calmly.

'What's up?' he asked.

'Oh—I've been rather sick and had an awful headache,' she said. 'It's nothing. Come up and have some tea.'

'Thanks.' Philip followed her up the stairs. She moved slowly, like an old woman, holding the rope that ran up the side as a banister.

'I'll make the tea,' said Philip firmly when they reached the top of the staircase. He propelled her into the sitting-room. 'You sit down and put your feet up.'

She was in no condition to protest, and collapsed back into the chair in front of the electric fire from which she had dragged herself to open the door.

Philip went into the kitchen and hunted about for the teapot and some cups. A dirty glass that had obviously held milk stood on the draining-board, beside a plate with the crumbs from some toast still on it; Penelope's lunch. He plugged in the electric kettle and switched it on, and found a loaf of bread from which he cut and buttered several slices and arranged them on a plate. Then he found a tin marked

TEA which proved to be empty except for a few dry leaves at the bottom, but a further search yielded a new packet in a cupboard. There was a bottle of milk in the refrigerator, and soon he had a tray prepared which he carried through into the sitting-room.

'Oh Philip, you are a dear,' said Penelope gratefully.

'There wasn't any tea in the tin, I opened a fresh packet and filled it up,' he said.

'Oh, that's right. I finished the other up yesterday,' she said.

Philip poured out and stood over her while she drank a cup of tea and ate some of the bread-and-butter. She began to revive a little, and he told her how he had spent the morning in Fleet Street, trying to be funny about his interview and make her laugh. Meanwhile he looked about the room. There was no sign of the other doll: he tried to think of a way of asking about it.

'How long have you been off colour, Penny?' he asked, when after a second cup of tea she declared she felt better.

'Oh, a week or so—it seems ages. Four or five days, I suppose,' she said vaguely.

'Had the doctor?'

She shook her head. 'It wasn't bad enough. Besides, we haven't got a doctor here. We haven't been ill and needed one. I haven't had a temperature.'

Philip frowned. Vincent should not have been complacent about her when she was obviously far from well; he should have insisted on getting advice. He got up and took away her empty cup and saucer. It was green Wedgwood, a stock pattern that could be matched easily in any good china shop. In stacking the things back on the tray Philip contrived to drop it, and to cut himself as he gathered up the broken pieces of china.

'Oh Penny, I'm terribly sorry,' he said, mopping at his wound with his handkerchief. 'How awful to come to come to tea and smash up your crocks.'

'It doesn't matter about the cup,' she exclaimed, 'but your hand, you've cut yourself.'

'It's nothing,' he said, squeezing it surreptitiously to encourage the blood to flow.

'But it is!' She got up to peer at it.

'I don't think so,' he said, dabbing it. 'But perhaps if you had a bit of plaster, just to stop it dripping all over the place.'

'Yes of course, there's some in the bathroom, I'll fetch it,' she said.

'No—you stay here, I'll find it,' Philip said, pushing her gently back into the chair with his unwounded hand.

'It's in the cupboard,' Penelope said. 'Are you sure you can manage?'

'Perfectly sure. You stay there and let your tea settle,' said Philip.

He picked up the tray, and with his hand still wrapped in the handkerchief carried it out to the kitchen. Then he went up the stairs to the bathroom. It was small and bright, with a black-sided bath and red terry-towelling curtains. There was a small mirror-fronted cupboard on the wall above the basin. Philip opened it; it contained a large bottle of aspirins, Phillips toothpaste, Dettol and a tin of Elastoplast. He quickly removed a strip of dressing from the box and then went quietly out of the bathroom and back on to the landing. Two doors confronted him. The first, above the kitchen, opened into a small single bedroom, plainly furnished with a divan bed and chintz-skirted dressing-table. He opened the second door.

He saw the doll at once. It was on the window-sill, standing looking out at the street below. Philip went quickly across the carpet, hoping his footsteps would not vibrate over Penelope's head as she sat in the room underneath. He lifted it up. The green velvet dress, low-cut, with small cap sleeves, was quite unlike the costume of any of the dolls in the shop, but the diminutive silk petticoat and little pants were the same. He looked at the face: it was identical with the one he had bought, but the wig was cut short, the smooth curls arranged close to the head. Plaits could be trimmed on people, so why not on dolls too?'

He replaced the doll carefully and went quietly out of the room.

'Did you manage?' Penelope asked when he entered the sitting-room again.

'Yes, thanks.' Philip had wrapped the strip of plaster round his cut as he hurried downstairs. 'It was stupid of me, I'm awfully sorry about the cup, Penny, I'll get you another.'

'Don't worry about it,' she said. 'I'm always smashing things. I never used to be a breaker but I am now.'

'Why don't you go down to Greyfriars for a few days?' said Philip. 'You don't look well, Penny. It would do you good to have a bit of a rest—let Queenie look after you. You're still fretting about Great-Aunt Hermione.'

'No—I'm not really—not more than you are,' she said. 'I've just had rather a bad few weeks lately, what with being sick and nearly getting run over.'

She suddenly found herself telling Philip about her misfortunes and how she had fallen off the bus.

'My own fault—clumsy as usual,' she said, attempting to laugh. 'Maybe I'm accident-prone.'

'No such thing,' said Philip stoutly. 'Look at what you did as a kid—climbing over the roofs and up trees —most children would have broken all their arms and legs dozens of times doing the things you used to do. You only concussed yourself once.'

Penelope remembered another day when she had crossed the roof at Greyfriars. Up she had gone, along the guttering, across the tiles and over the apex at the top, then scrambled down the other side, a dare she had given herself. Queenie, below, coming out by chance to witness the deed, had been green with fright till she reached the ground and had scolded her furiously. Great-Aunt Hermione had laughed and praised the action, but forbidden its repetition.

'Your nerves are a bit unstrung, love,' Philip said, bringing her back to the present. 'It was all so sudden and horrible, at Christmas, it was enough to unman anyone. I should pop down to Greyfriars for a bit. Vincent wouldn't mind, would he?' He managed to utter the name.

She wondered. He couldn't be finding her much of an asset at present, for ever ailing, but she felt that she ought not to leave him. The idea of a week at Greyfriars seemed like a prospect of heaven to her, and she was horrified to find that she thought so. If Vincent had suggested leaving her alone while he took a week's holiday she would be bitterly hurt: or would she? Would she not clutch at the respite? She blinked.

'I'll think about it,' she promised.

Philip rose reluctantly to go.

'Are you sure you're all right?' he asked. He hated to leave her, but there was no time to lose.

'Yes, really,' she assured him. 'I feel much better. It was nice of you to come.'

'I'll let myself out,' said Philip. 'Don't you come down.'

She heard him going down the stairs and the bang as he closed the front door. Then came the sound of his car starting up. Penelope went to the window and watched him turn and drive off. She could see his red head sticking up out of the car; he still had the hood down, his only concession to winter being a thick muffler flung round his neck. There went a friend.

She felt solitary and forlorn as she turned back to the empty room. The little ivory ship on the mantelpiece caught her eye and she picked it up. A wave of giddiness hit her as she stood there, holding it. When it had passed she went upstairs, still holding the ship. At the top she debated; would she be sick or was it safe to lie down? She decided it was, and went into her room. Her glance flew at once to the doll. It stood where she had left it, on the window-sill, looking out at the street.

Penelope went over to it and put the ship down on the painted woodwork beside the small, menacing figure in green.

11

Philip drove from Penelope's house in Kensington straight to Automobile Kings, Ltd., off Piccadilly. He parked his car in a side street and then walked down towards the magnificent premises occupied by the firm that employed Vincent. Through the colossal windows he could see Rolls Royces, Daimlers and Bentleys, Lagondas, and all the most luxurious makes of cars glistening with newness among potted palms and debonair young men in black coats and striped trousers. He pushed open the swing doors and went in. A slim, pale young man with black hair and a toothbrush moustache approached.

Philip tried to look rich.

'Have you the new model M.G.?' he asked. 'I have a 1955 two-seater I was thinking of turning in. I haven't seen the new ones—just got back from the States.' He thought this admission might lend him tone.

'I'm afraid we don't deal with M.G.'s, except for special orders,' said the salesman discouragingly. 'I'd have to enquire about delivery times.' He was the sort of suave young man who made Philip feel provincial and young, though they were both much of a size and of similar age.

'Oh—the new Bermuda.' Philip's eye lit on a maroon-coloured, torpedo-like sports car tucked into a corner. 'May I look at it?'

'But of course.' The young man knew very well that he could never sell Philip a Bermuda, and that his approach to the car was much that of a woman with ten minutes to spare trying on hats just for fun. Wearily he demonstrated the points of the car. Philip knew a lot about the internal-combustion engine and talked intelligently to the salesman, while he glanced about hoping for a sight of Vincent. There were doors concealing offices in the background, and other willowy young men who drifted about in an expectant way waiting for customers, but no Vincent.

'What about secondhand cars? Do you have any?' asked Philip.

'Oh yes—round at the back,' said the salesman.

'May I see what you've got?' asked Philip. He was now aware that the young man had guessed the state of his bank balance and that he was merely a frivolous enquirer, but he was dogged. Reluctantly the salesman led him through the showrooms, past glass-windowed offices, into the rear of the building where grease-covered mechanics were working. By now Philip would not have been surprised to recognize Vincent among them, but he did not. About twenty used cars, all clean and shining, were parked in neat rows at one side of the workshop. Philip and the young man walked along, looking at them. There was one M.G. like Philip's own, cream-coloured, several large saloons including a Rover and some Austins, and at the end of one line a big black Humber.

Philip made his excuses and left by the door at the back which opened into an alley.

Thinking hard, he went back to the street where his own car was parked. If Vincent wanted to surprise Penelope by giving her a doll that looked like herself why did he pretend to have bought it in the King's Road when he had got it in a shop just off Bond Street? It was too much of a coincidence, surely, that a man so like Vincent should have bought two dolls from the blonde girl with the eye-shadow so lately. But assuming that it was Vincent, why had he lied to the assistant and told her that he was a widower with a small daughter? What had given him the idea of changing the doll's dress, and how had he contrived to do it?

No. It was his over-active imagination twisting things round. There must be a second shop in the King's Road which dealt in the dolls, but dressed them in current fashions. The rest was chance. But all the same it was worrying. Why keep the pieces of doll? He would come up to London again as soon as he could and explore the King's Road for doll shops.

The fact of Penelope's evident illness disturbed him. She was anxious and unhappy, he was sure; the tale of her misadventures showed she was not in a condition to concentrate. What was Vincent thinking of to let her go on like this without doing something about it? To and fro, round and round, went Philip's thoughts.

Why lie? In his heart Philip was sure it was Vincent who had bought the dolls from the shop he had visited this morning. If everything was fair, square and above-board why fabricate?

He brooded as he drove along the road out of London, through Bagshot and Camberley. Instinct told him something was very wrong although he could not prove it. When he reached the side turning which Vincent and Penelope had taken on Christmas Eve to go to Foxbourne St. Mary he too turned off, and was soon driving along the narrow country lanes. Instead of turning left at the bottom of the hill to reach his own home three miles further on, Philip swung the car round in the direction of Greyfriars. He drove slowly up the short drive. At the top, in the darkness, the house loomed, a solid mass against the night sky.

There was no light burning in the front. Philip rang the bell and waited, stamping his cold feet on the step. The house remained silent. He rang again, and this time when there was no reply he walked round to the back of the building where Queenie and Cartwright had their rooms. There was no lighted window on this side of the house either. Philip frowned. The Cartwrights must have gone to the cinema. He strolled round to the garage where Cartwright kept his old prewar Ford. The door was shut and locked: how cautious. Philip went on round the yard and back to his own car.

Very soon he was home, and late for dinner which annoyed his mother. His father was out at an emergency case, and they sat alone together in the panelled dining-room eating lamb chops, while Dr Torrington's helping languished in the oven till at last he returned.

Philip related the story of his success in Fleet Street, and his mother was soon won back to good humour. When they had finished discussing how many copies of his novel would sell and how soon he might expect fame, Philip asked: 'Tell me about that chap Penelope's married. Who is he?'

'Well—I don't know a lot about him,' said Mrs Torrington. 'He's an old friend of Fred Tompkins—he stayed with Fred for Easter last year, and met Penny at a party. He has some very good job with a car firm in London. Mrs Vandyk was pleased about it.'

'Hm.' Philip digested this. 'What's your view?' he asked.

'Well,' she said, 'frankly I thought Penelope was too young to get married after knowing him so short a time. He's much older than she—fourteen years, if not more.'

'Do you think age is so important?' asked Philip abstractedly.

'Not if everything else is right,' said Mrs Torrington. 'But Penelope hadn't long to get to know him, and meeting at parties or dining out in London isn't the best way of discovering if you're suited for life.' She looked shrewdly at her son, but he was too intent upon his questions to notice.

'Why didn't Aunt Hermione think that?' asked Philip, to whom this seemed reasonable.

'I was rather surprised at her attitude,' said Mrs Torrington. 'She seemed to welcome it. I think she knew she hadn't long to live, and she wanted to see Penelope settled. I never said anything to disquieten her. In any case when two people have made up their minds to get married nothing on earth will dissuade them. But why all this interest, Philip?' Perhaps he would tell her something she was afraid to hear.

'I don't know.' Philip drew pictures on his side plate with the handle of his knife. 'I popped in to see Penny this afternoon, and she wasn't very well. She'd been sick and looked wretched.'

'Oh dear.' Mrs Torrington looked concerned.

'I think she's still brooding about the old lady,' said Philip. 'That was a bad business—merciful, I suppose, but such a shock and so beastly. I'll drop in and see her again in a day or two, next time I go up. I suppose that chap looks after her properly.'

'I expect so, dear,' said his mother. She looked at her son compassionately. She had been afraid of this.

‘I’ll have to see about finding somewhere to live in London,’ Philip was saying. ‘I think I shall be able to land one or two weekly columns, and I must be on the spot.’

‘Of course, dear.’ Mrs Torrington had made the most of these weeks when Philip had been at home; all good things, she knew, came to an end only too soon. She sighed.

In the morning Philip went round again to Greyfriars; Queenie and Cartwright were sure to be at home at this time. He rang the bell, as he had done the previous night, and again there was no answer. Once more he strode round to the back of the house. It seemed deserted: every window was closed, and when he peered through the kitchen window there was no sign of life to be observed within. Now thoroughly alarmed, Philip got back into his car and drove up the village to the Post Office, where he drew up with a jerk, slammed the door of the car shut and walked up the cobbled path to the small thatched cottage where Miss Prewett combined a small confectionery business with the management of the Queen’s postal affairs.

She was a small grey-haired woman, neat and quick. She was pleased to see Philip, whom she remembered as a boy buying gob-stoppers and liquorice, and he was forced to tell her about his travels in America before he could broach the real reason for his visit.

‘I’ve just been up to Greyfriars,’ he said at last. ‘Thought I’d like a chat with Mrs Cartwright, but the place seems deserted.’

‘Oh, hadn’t you heard?’ Miss Prewett clucked her tongue behind her dentures. ‘Terrible about the old lady, wasn’t it? Still a mercy in some ways, poor old soul. Gone in a flash, they say.’

‘Yes, very sad,’ said Philip impatiently.

'You were there at the time, of course, I was forgetting,' said Miss Prewett. 'Still, I thought your father would have heard about the Cartwrights.'

'What about them, Miss Prewett?' Philip asked, grinding his teeth to himself. 'We've heard nothing.'

'I never would have believed it of Miss Penelope,' said Miss Prewett, shaking her head sadly. 'Given them their notice, she has. At least, the lawyers wrote to them saying they wouldn't be needed any more as the house was to be sold, and they had orders to go by the end of last week. Queenie took on something awful about it, I can tell you. She was very upset at Miss Penny not telling her herself. Didn't like to, I suppose, and I don't wonder after all those years. Fancy turning them out like that so quick. Seems Penny doesn't want to come down here any more after what happened. Only natural, I suppose. That Mr Dereham's very likely at the bottom of it, I never could take to him though he seemed such a nicely-spoken gentleman.'

None of this tied up with the conversation Philip had had with Penelope only the day before; she had said nothing about the sale of Greyfriars or about sending the Cartwrights away. Surely she would have told him if she had known? Vincent and the lawyers must have made the arrangements without reference to her; they had no business to do so even if they did intend to spare her feelings.

Philip resisted the urge to pursue the interesting topic of Miss Prewett's antipathy to Vincent, and he reminded himself that she was notoriously an unreliable source of news, but she seemed sure enough about the Cartwrights.

'Where have they gone?' he demanded. 'Do you know?'

'Oh yes—they've gone up to Scotland to visit Mr Cartwright's old mother. Ninety, she is, and still gets about.

Wonderful how some people carry on, isn't it?' said Miss Prewett.

'Yes, indeed,' said Philip. 'You wouldn't have their address, by any chance?'

'Oh yes, I have it here. Of course they filled in a form for the re-direction of post, but I had it in case anything slipped past by mistake,' said Miss Prewett. She hunted through a pile of papers and finally found what she sought. Philip waited while she wrote the address slowly down. It was in Edinburgh, he saw, reading it upside down as she laboriously printed it.

He hurried out of the Post Office, promising to come and see Miss Prewett again soon, and drove up the road, past the church, to the whitewashed Georgian house where Major Tompkins lived.

The Major was out in the cold February air inspecting his vegetables, a depressing spectacle at this time of the year, limp and drooping with wet. At his heels loped a black spaniel.

'Oh—' morning, Philip,' said the Major, pleased to have a visitor. He led him at once into his study, where a stove made the room welcomingly warm after the chill outside.

Again Philip had to spend some time in idle smalltalk before he could steer the conversation round to Vincent. He told the story of his book and his efforts in Fleet Street, and finally said: 'I went to see Penelope while I was in London. She's not too well, poor thing.'

'Oh dear. Nothing serious, I hope?' Major Tompkins was distressed. His white eyebrows were raised anxiously into crescents.

'A chill, I expect,' said Philip. He paused, wondering how to phrase his next remark. 'Have you known Dereham long?' he asked bluntly, at last.

'Funny you should ask that,' said Major Tompkins. 'I was only thinking about it this morning. No—we were together in Africa for a bit—he was seconded to me for a time—pleasant enough chap. I ran into him at Hurst Park last year, and he seemed at a bit of a loose end so I asked him down—rather in an idle moment, as you might say, never thought he'd take it literally. I said "Come down sometime," d'ye know, or something of the sort, and next thing I knew he was here for Easter.' He laughed. 'Then he goes and sweeps off little Penny. Funny how things work out.'

Funny indeed, thought Philip, furiously.

'I was thinking about him today because of the Cartwrights,' went on Major Tompkins. 'A sad business, that—not like Penny to do that sort of thing secondhand. Dereham wrote the letter and sent the cheque.'

'Not the solicitor?'

'Oh no. Poor Queenie was in tears—a good soul. Couldn't believe Penny didn't want her.'

Nor could Philip. He remembered Queenie on the night Great-Aunt Hermione died, fussing round Penelope and calming her. He walked slowly back to his car thinking of how through the years she had comforted Penelope and cared for her. He remembered the doll, that night, sitting on the dressing-table, and Penny's pale face on the pillow. His own doll, the one he had bought the day before, was still in the car. He looked at it thoughtfully.

Then he seemed to hear in his head Major Tompkins' voice:

'Mind you take care of it. Don't want to go sticking any pins in it, do you?'

12

Penelope had slept so little lately that when she woke suddenly it was a surprise to discover she had at last been sleeping. The house was still and silent: outside there was no sound of traffic in the quiet street, and the pale glimmer from the street lamps sent shafts of silver through the parted curtains. Her head was aching and she was thirsty. She stretched wearily: she was so tired.

Vincent had made her have supper in bed that evening, when he came home from work and found her still lying down. He had brought her a cup of Bovril, and scrambled eggs on toast, which she had forced herself to eat. It had all been rather salty, and she supposed that was why she now felt such an acute thirst. It would have been ungrateful not to have made the effort to get through what he had prepared for her with such kindness, before he grilled himself a steak. Penelope had managed to ring up the butcher before she collapsed that morning, but she felt increasingly guilty that Vincent should have to set to and cook every evening after his work because she was not well.

Weak with sickness, and lightheaded from a series of wakeful nights punctured with troubled dreams, Penelope lay between the sheets trying to ignore the dryness in her throat. Beside her, in the other bed, Vincent was motionless, a hump, snoring slightly. She slid cautiously out on to the floor and crossed over to the window, wrapping her thick quilted dressing-gown round her. The china doll still looked out, unblinking, at the street. Penelope laid her hand briefly on the little ship. Her head thumped, and her lips felt parched. She pattered out on to the landing and went into the bathroom in search of aspirins and a drink of water. When she pulled the string that worked the light switch there was a faint click, but otherwise nothing happened; the bulb must have gone. She groped about for the tooth-mug, but could not find it in the darkness. That was odd: she had used it earlier in the evening and put it back in the chromium ring fixed to the wall where it lived. She could feel the ring, empty now; she hunted about, her fingers searching for it on the window-sill and on the shelf by the bath, but without success. There was nothing for it but to go downstairs to the kitchen.

Penelope came out of the bathroom on to the landing again. She felt along the wall for the light switch at the top of the stairs, but when she pressed it, once again, apart from the click it made, nothing happened. This bulb must have gone too. She had not put on the landing light when she came out of her room in case it woke Vincent by shining in through the half-closed door, but now she tried it, only to meet again with no response. A fuse must have blown, and all three lights were sure to be on the same one, she thought. She crept back into the bedroom and tried to find the small torch which always lived on the table beside her, but it was not there. She was tempted to abandon her search for a drink of water, but she knew she was so thirsty that there would be no hope of further sleep if she did. She went back again on to the landing and began gingerly to descend, feeling the way with her slippered feet, a hand on the wall at either side of her. After the first few treads she went on with more confidence, her eyes screwed up in an attempt to pierce the darkness, until all at once her balance went and she fell with sickening suddenness, bumping down the rest of the way. She tried to stop her fall, hands outstretched to grasp any support, but she went on till she came to the last stair. She lay there, moaning a little, her body bruised and aching and her heart thumping. Tears stung her eyes; she had banged both shins hard in her precipitous descent, and she could not begin to rise at first because of the pain and shock. She crouched there, rubbing her legs, and rocking back and forth uttering small sounds of distress which stopped her from hearing Vincent's approach. Suddenly he was beside her, helping her up, asking where she was hurt, and full of concern and distress. When he was assured that no bones were broken he carried her upstairs again, still in the darkness, but with light streaming out from the bedroom on to the landing.

Vincent made her move every limb to make quite certain there was no serious damage. Her fall had not been a long one; the fright it had given her was its worst result.

'I was getting a drink,' she told him, sobbing, but in a shocked way, without tears.

'But why didn't you get one from the bathroom?' he asked. 'Why go downstairs?'

'I couldn't find the mug—and I wanted an aspirin—the light wouldn't work,' she said.

'I'll get you a drink,' said Vincent. He went out of the room, pulling the door shut behind him, and she heard him moving about in the bathroom opposite.

'The mug was there, in the ring on the wall,' he said when he returned a few minutes later carrying it filled with water, and with the aspirin bottle in his other hand.

'But it couldn't have been, I felt for it, the ring was empty,' Penelope said.

'It was there,' Vincent repeated. 'And the light is quite all right now. Are you sure you turned it on?'

'Yes, yes,' she insisted. 'I tried all the switches—the landing and the stairs ones too. None of them worked.'

'I don't think you did, dear,' he said. 'They're all working perfectly now.'

'I did—I know I did,' she declared.

'Well, you haven't been quite yourself lately, have you?' said Vincent gently. 'Don't worry about it—perhaps there was a power cut just while you were out of bed. Forget it. Here's your drink.'

She took the mug from him. Her hand shook as she swallowed down the three aspirins he gave her and then drank.

'You must be more careful, my dear,' he said in an admonitory tone, standing above her. 'You haven't been well, I know, but it's mostly a question of nerves. You've been thinking too much about your mother and it's preying on your mind. Perhaps I shouldn't have told you about her. Pull yourself together, Penelope. You've been having too many accidents. It's all due to carelessness, you know.'

'Yes, Vincent.' Her voice was a whisper.

He went away with the mug, and she turned on her side, facing the wall. Vincent came back, switched out the light and got into bed. Soon she heard the regular breathing which indicated that he slept.

She rolled on to her back and stared up in the darkness at the ceiling. She ached all over; the pain in her head had lessened because it had so much to compete with, but in addition to her bruises she felt aware of every nerve in her body. She seemed to prick all over with tenseness and horror. She began to think she must be going mad. She had groped round everywhere in the bathroom for the plastic mug; it had not been there, yet Vincent had found it in the ring where it belonged. The lights had worked for Vincent but not for her. She had fallen off a bus through her own folly; she had nearly been run over by a black Humber although because it mounted the kerb her own carelessness could hardly in this case be blamed. She had been sick and ailing for days with no clear explanation of the cause, and now she had fallen downstairs.

As she slid at last over the boundary into sleep Penelope thought back to the moment when she was descending the stairs: her feet inched down, one step at a time, and she felt again the unexplained thing that had nagged at her mind under its preoccupation with the more immediate problem of pain, the sensation of something soft stretched against the thick padded silk of her dressing-gown above her ankle, something that hampered her passage and made her fall.

In the morning her feeling of sickness had gone but she was sore in every limb. She got up and made tea, determined to take Vincent's words to heart and control herself. She cooked eggs and bacon for his breakfast, and ate two pieces of toast herself. When he left for the office she forced herself to wash up and clean the house thoroughly before admitting that she still felt exhausted.

When she ceased her activity fear returned. All her short life so far had been secure and happy: she had never before felt lost and out on a limb on her own, and she could not understand what had happened to her. The thought of her mother kept haunting her; and the little doll in its green dress mesmerized her so that she felt drawn to look at it, unable to ignore its compelling presence in the house, and the vague sense of threat it seemed to hold.

What had she?

Vincent.

It would be all right, she knew it would. This was the adjusting time people talked about, and if she could only feel well again and stop being frightened everything would be all right. But she didn't feel well, and she was afraid, desperately afraid of something she could not describe.

Vincent had told her she was not to telephone him at his work, but surely her present panic made an exception: she needed him. She must have reassurance.

She took the telephone directory out of the drawer where it lived and looked up the number of Automobile Kings, Ltd. It rang three times after she had dialled it, before a girl's voice answered: 'Automobile Kings, Ltd. Good-morning. Can I help you?'

'Could I speak to Mr Dereham, please?' Penelope asked, trying to keep her voice steady. In a minute Vincent would answer: she would hear his even tones; she would be calm, and just ask him to come home because she wasn't well. She must go down to Greyfriars to get better. Only a minute now while they switched her through, and then she would hear him.

'Mr Dereham?' The voice at the other end sounded bewildered. 'Would you spell it please?'

Penelope did so. 'Mr Vincent Dereham —the director,' she added.

There was a pause.

'I'm afraid you must have the wrong number, caller,' said the voice smoothly. 'This is Automobile Kings, Ltd., Mayfair. We have no Mr Dereham on our staff.'

13

'We have no Mr Dereham on our staff.'

As she put the receiver down the words seemed to echo in Penelope's ears.

She was out of her mind, of course. Vincent must work somewhere else. Another Automobile Kings, perhaps. She searched in the telephone directory, but there was no other firm of that name. She sat down in one of the big arm-chairs, her hand to her head, trying to control her racing thoughts and to think calmly. She took several deep breaths.

She was Penelope Dereham, aged nearly nineteen, married to Vincent Dereham aged thirty-two, late of Her Majesty's Army and currently a director of Automobile Kings, Ltd., Mayfair, full stop.

But he must be there! She got up and went again to the telephone, but before she dialled the number for a second time she changed her mind. He had told her not to ring him up. Was the reason because he was too busy, as he implied, for time-wasting calls, or was it because he had lost his job and was afraid to tell her? Yes, that must be the explanation. She felt more assured after coming to that conclusion. She sat still for a few more minutes, trying to still the frenzied thoughts that poured into her brain. Why had he not told her? What little confidence he had in her not to disclose the disaster. It showed how much she had failed him.

Presently she got to her feet and went slowly upstairs. In the bathroom the tooth-mug was again in its ring on the wall. She put her hand on it and closed her eyes. She could not have imagined that it was not there last night: that was real, it had gone. But Vincent had found it.

She went across the landing and into the bedroom. As if by a magnet she was drawn across to the window where the doll stood upon the sill. She looked down at the little, delicate china creature. She picked it up slowly and turned it so that the face was uppermost. The eyes stared at her, and she tilted it back till they closed. She saw the small flaw on the shin, and felt the ache of the old bruise among the fresh ones on her own. The memory of the other mark, the tiny crack on the doll's body over the heart, came to her. She set it down again and rushed over to the door; she ran down the stairs, gasping, till she reached the bottom. Suddenly the little house, once so charming, seemed filled with menace. Horror pressed upon her: she was doomed.

She seized her thick tweed coat from its peg under the stairs and hurried out, slamming the front door shut behind her. Hands in her pockets, she walked down the mews as fast as she could, away from the aura of threat. It was a foggy day, and the air was damp and clammy. Buses and cars loomed up out of the mist, blowing their horns furiously when she crossed blindly in front of them.

She walked and walked, not knowing or caring where she went, till the morning passed and afternoon came. Her hair, uncovered, was damp and clung to her skull: her hands, although thrust into her pockets, were icy. In her mind her only thought was of her mother: in imagination she saw a pale, fragile creature stretching out a transparent hand to lift up a glass of water that was cloudy like milk. 'A time to die.' The words drummed in Penelope's ears. She had missed death narrowly out in the street: twice she had fallen, and if less lucky might well have been killed or at least badly hurt. She had been unwell, sick and exhausted, for days. 'If it's coming to you, it's coming.' She had heard that said too, before.

She walked on blindly, brain in a tumult, until she came to a bridge.

It was Westminster Bridge. She did not recognize it in the mist and in her confused state of mind. She stopped and stared over the side at the river, only just visible below. It looked grey and cold. In the distance sirens hooted with a melancholy note as tugs steamed up and down through the fog. Behind her the traffic rumbled. There were few pedestrians; the weather was cruel enough to keep all who could stay there indoors. Penelope gazed down at the water so far below. It was swirling with the tide. It would be a short fall, soon over: then the gasping lungs would shrink with the chill of the water. Her heavy coat would drag her down. If she was meant to die, here was the way. It seemed so easy, just a moment to climb the parapet and jump. No one would see her, if she waited and chose her time. Better this, by far, than to go on being sick, or to be run over properly. She put out her hand and touched the bridge. It was cold and damp. Her head throbbed: that would end, that incessant headache, and the nausea with it. There would be a moment's struggle, perhaps; then a blank, peace, and an end to fear. She took a step forward and placed her other hand on the bridge.

Suddenly, as if someone had shaken her, Penelope came to herself. Her head cleared and her eyes focussed. She found herself standing on the bridge looking down at the water below and knew that she had seriously contemplated casting herself into it because she was afraid of her life. She took several backward steps, her heart beating fast, appalled at what had come over her.

It was a devil: it was the devil in the doll, the devil that made her clumsy and careless, so that she fell over, nearly got run over, and became ill. It was a devil that had driven away her own good sense. She moved away from the parapet and walked, not very steadily, along the path to the end of it. On her left the Houses of Parliament loomed ghostly in the fog. She crossed the road carefully, making sure that the traffic had stopped, and entered the Abbey.

Just inside she sat down. It was very quiet, and almost empty. It seemed very light and clear after the fog in the atmosphere outside, though even here a small haze had penetrated. Penelope sat and waited, and presently she began to think.

No doll could possibly portend her doom. She had been shocked by Great-Aunt Hermione's death and had allowed her imagination to run riot. The fact that her own mother had ended her life was pathetic and frightening, but important now only as a warning that she must come to terms with her own problems and not run away from them. She was horrified at what she had nearly done, but she remembered what lack of sleep had done to the Macbeths.

After a time she got up and went out of the Abbey, intending to catch a bus home. It was only then that she realized she had come out with no money, and without a key to let herself in when she did get back.

Perhaps Vincent —. But she could not go back with him. She did not know where to find him.

She walked all the way back, along Whitehall, down the Mall, out at Hyde Park Corner and on through the Park till she reached the end of the gardens, crossed the square and came to the corner with the old withered tree that served as a landmark and turned down into the mews. The door was shut, just as she had left it. She leaned against it, swaying with exhaustion, wondering what to do, and then Vincent drove up in his Vauxhall.

Penelope took a deep breath. She felt strangely detached, concentrating on keeping in command of herself. He got out of the car and came round to her. She turned her head abruptly, suddenly fearing that he might kiss her.

'I—I've—hullo, Vincent,' she said, rather breathlessly. 'I've been out for a walk—I forgot my key.'

'Silly girl,' he chided her. 'You must try to control your memory—you'll forget yourself next,' he said mildly, fitting his own key into the lock. Vincent never mislaid his possessions.

She almost told him how nearly she had done exactly that, but refrained.

He stood back for her to enter the house in front of him, and she went into the narrow hall. Her coat was soaked, and she went straight upstairs with it to hang it over the hot rail in the bathroom. Then she towelled her hair briskly till it was nearly dry.

Vincent had gone straight into the sitting-room and was reading the evening paper, turned to the racing news.

Penelope came downstairs again. Her mind was icily calm; she was aware of the fact that she was ravenously hungry and had made no preparations for dinner. She fried eggs and bacon and made tea; the blue tin where it lived was full, for Philip had yesterday emptied the new packet into it. She laid a tray for Vincent with his loaded plate; a cup and saucer, and two bananas; some bread, butter and cheese, and carried it in to him.

'I don't want much,' she told him glibly. 'I'll have it in a minute—my hair's still rather wet and I'm going to dry it first.'

'Oh, very well, my dear,' he said in the humouring voice he had used lately. 'I'll bring you some hot milk later.'

'No, not tonight, thank you, Vincent,' she said. 'I don't want any.'

'Just as you say, Penelope,' he said, turning a page of his paper.

She went back to the kitchen, closed the door, and quickly ate her own helping of bacon and egg, drank three cups of tea with plenty of sugar, and ate two bananas herself. Then she washed up the evidence of her large meal before he could find her amongst it and hurried upstairs.

She had a very hot bath, washed her fog-damp hair and thoroughly rubbed it again. Then she went into the bedroom. She picked up the doll: it still looked like her, but she no longer feared it. She laid it on Vincent's bed, then thought better of that and replaced it on the window-sill. She looked at Philip's little ivory boat: he, anyway, she trusted.

Penelope never knew what it was that impelled her suddenly to go over to the door where Vincent's red silk dressing-gown hung on a hook and look in the pocket.

From it she drew slowly a piece of wide white tape, about a yard long, with two small holes pierced at each end, and four drawing pins.

14

Vincent left for work at nine o'clock as usual the next morning. As soon as the car had disappeared round the corner at the end of the mews where the old tree drooped over the railings Penelope emerged from the house. She had put on an old camel coat that she seldom wore; this time she carried her handbag and did not forget the front-door key. She ran down the road to the corner: the Vauxhall could just be seen in the distance, rapidly disappearing. She hurried after it, and luck was with her when a cruising taxi came up behind her almost immediately.

'That Vauxhall—the black one up there—please follow it,' she gasped, tumbling into the cab.

With a jerk of his clutch the driver slid into gear and started off; he roared up the road and was soon sitting close behind Vincent, parted from him by only four other cars. The traffic grew thicker when they left the quiet residential streets, and Penelope's taxi had no difficulty in keeping the quarry in sight. Vincent went on, turned left into the Park, and went round over the Serpentine. All the way the taxi followed, with Penelope sitting upright in the back, leaning forward a little to look out through the windscreen, beside the burly back of the driver. On they went, and left the Park to cross the Bayswater Road and penetrate the labyrinth of streets which lay beyond. Left and right they turned, and then the Vauxhall stopped outside a house. Penelope spoke urgently.

'Drive on, please,' she told the driver.

He obeyed, and she sat back as they passed. Vincent was getting out. There he was, a familiar stranger, shutting the car door as Penelope drove by. She turned, when they had gone past, and peered through the small window in the back of the taxi to watch him. She saw him run quickly up the steps of the house outside which he had stopped, and put a key in the lock.

At the end of the road Penelope told her driver to turn and drive slowly back past the Vauxhall again. He did so, and she saw the closed black front door of the house: Number Fifteen, Sycamore Gardens. She felt she would never forget that address.

She paid off the taxi when they had gone into the Park again, and sat down on a bench overlooking the Serpentine. It was very cold, but the fog of the previous day had gone. A few ducks swam hopefully up, and when they discovered she had no crusts for them departed again for a more promising spot further along the bank.

Her mind still would not accept the discovery of the tape in Vincent's dressing-gown pocket. She remembered her fall downstairs, and the feeling of something soft pressing against her leg, but she refused to recognize the connection. He had lost his job with Automobile Kings, Ltd., and had found another, not so good, in Sycamore Gardens. He had not dared to tell her of the change.

She put her hands to her head. The clarity of thought she had suddenly captured yesterday on Westminster Bridge came back to her: steadily she looked at the months of her life with Vincent: at the queer, indefinable disappointment; the restless, insecure feeling she had discovered instead of tranquillity. She remembered the presents he had given her; and the attentions he had lavished on her when she felt ill, never complaining because she was not undertaking her full share of their divided load. She remembered his gift of the doll; and the terrible story he had told her about her mother. He had lied to her about his work: had he lied about other things too?

After a time she rose and found another taxi. She drove once more past the house in Sycamore Gardens, turned at the end of the road and came back. The last time, as she passed, she saw Vincent emerge from the house. He was not alone. With him was a woman, tall and blonde, dressed in green. In the second while she looked at her Penelope knew she had seen her before, but she could not remember where. They got into the Vauxhall together, and looking back, Penelope saw them drive away.

She got her taxi to take her to Betty's house in Chelsea.

Betty had just put the baby in the pram in the little back garden after her bath and feed. A woman with a duster tied round her head was operating a Hoover in the hall, and small Stephen was playing with a toy farm on the nursery floor. The atmosphere of the house was comforting and normal. Penelope could not know that her face was grey, but when Betty had made her sit down by the fire she realized she was shaking.

'Whatever is wrong, Penny?' Betty's voice was full of anxiety, though she tried to appear calm. 'Have you nearly been run over again?'

'No.' Penelope shook her head.

'What is it? Tell me,' Betty coaxed. Inwardly she was panic-stricken; Penelope looked as if she was on the borderline of hysteria. 'Wait—don't talk for a minute,' she said, as Penelope seemed about to speak. 'I'll get you something to buck you up.' She hurried out of the room, and returned very quickly carrying a port glass full of brandy. 'Drink this, you're frozen and it will pull you together,' she said.

Obediently Penelope sipped the brandy, pulling a face as she swallowed it, but it warmed her and a little colour came back into her face.

'Now,' said Betty. 'What's up?'

'Well.' Penelope did not know where to begin. 'It's Vincent,' she said at last.

Betty was hardly surprised by this disclosure.

'What's he done?' she asked.

'He's thrown up his job, and I've just seen him drive off with a woman in his car,' said Penelope. Her voice shook.

This was more than Betty had anticipated. Words over breakfast or complaints about Penelope's cooking were all she had expected.

'Why's he thrown up his job?' she asked, beginning at the easier end of the problem.

'I don't know—he didn't tell me—he doesn't know I've found out.' The words began to tumble out now. 'I rang up Automobile Kings—he never said he'd left —I was sick and I wanted him—they said he didn't work there,' Penelope gasped. 'Then this morning I followed him. I got a taxi after he left and went after him. He drove to Sycamore Gardens, near Paddington, stopped at a house and went in. Number Fifteen, it was,' she said, as if the number was of special significance. 'Then later I went back and he came out with a woman and they drove off.'

Betty refused to accept circumstantial evidence.

'There's probably a perfectly reasonable explanation,' she said. 'Maybe she's a new secretary he's been interviewing, or an aunt, or something.'

'She didn't look like an aunt,' said Penelope. She took a deep breath. She wanted to tell Betty the whole story, about the doll, and the tape, and what they must mean, but she knew that she could not. It was too fantastic, too incredible. Betty was so practical, she would think Penelope had dreamed it all up in her imagination.

'Something must have happened at work that he felt he couldn't tell you about—some awful bit of bad luck,' said Betty now. 'Perhaps he didn't want to worry you when you were still upset about your aunt. He'll tell you when he's got it all straightened out.' She could not imagine Derek having a worry he would not want to share with her. 'Surely he knew you'd soon find out about the job—he must have realized you would as soon as you telephoned him?'

'He told me I wasn't to ring him up. He said he had so many conferences,' said Penelope dully.

Derek, if he ever had five minutes to spare in the day, often rang Betty up just for the pleasure of hearing her voice at the other end of the line. She was secure and loved; she knew, very clearly now and with a sinking heart, that Penelope was neither.

'There must be an explanation,' she repeated. She seldom telephoned Derek, because she respected his work too much to disturb him unnecessarily, but not because she was afraid. 'Look—you said you hadn't been well—why don't you stay here for a few days, he'll understand, and that will give you time to rest and think a bit. You look fagged out. Then you can talk to him about it. You'll be able to sort it out.'

'If it was only that,' said Penelope hopelessly. 'If it was only that he'd lost his job and been frightened to tell me. But directors don't lose their jobs so easily. There's much more to it than that.'

'You aren't happy with him,' Betty said.

Penelope shook her head. The relief of admitting it was enormous. 'I thought it would get better,' she said. 'But it hasn't. He's very good to me—he does things for me,' she added quickly.

'You poor little kid,' said Betty. She did not know what to say. She could not advise Penelope to cut and run after so short a time and knowing so few facts. There must be much that was undisclosed. If, however, the woman that Penelope had seen with Vincent was in fact not a secretary or business acquaintance the matter might in time resolve itself.

Penelope got up slowly. 'I feel better for telling someone,' she said. 'I must go back now,' she went on, with sudden dignity. 'I never washed up or anything this morning. I'll ask him tonight where he's working.'

Betty could think of no alternative suggestion. She rose too.

'You're sure? Do you feel all right now?' she asked anxiously.

Penelope nodded.

'Well, you know you can come here any time, for as long as you like, day or night,' said Betty. 'You won't hesitate, will you Penny? If you're miserable or ill? Just turn up, or we'll come for you. Maybe Derek could help, he's awfully wise.' She wished he was here now, her solid, reliable young husband who had clear ideas about every problem he met.

'No—I won't—I mean, yes I will,' said Penelope. 'Thank you, Betty. I'm sorry to be such a pest.'

'Don't be silly,' said Betty, hugging her.

Penelope went back on the bus. As she alighted she remembered where she had seen Vincent's companion, the woman with blonde hair. It was she who had helped her when she fell off the bus on that other occasion two weeks before. She had carried a long umbrella with a handle shaped like the head of a bird, and with a long, fresh scratch on the beak.

15

It was dark when Philip's plane taxied smoothly down the runway at the airport just outside Edinburgh. Soon he was driving through the wide streets into the city. Up here it was much colder, and a crust of snow lay on the buildings. His taxi took him round the suburbs to a quiet road high above the Firth of Forth, and stopped outside a grey stone semi-detached house. Philip asked the driver to wait, and walked quickly up the path to the front door. A salt breeze from the Forth blew hard against him as he waited for the bell to be answered, and his overcoat flapped round his legs, whipped by the force of it. His hair was swept by it, and his face under the untidy red thatch looked extraordinarily youthful to the plump woman who opened the door and gazed enquiringly out at him.

The wind scurried past Philip into the house, blowing through the narrow hall where he could see an elaborate carved hat-rack and coat-stand which jutted from the wall half-way across what little space there was. The floor was covered in brown linoleum, with a tatting rug islanded in the centre; and beyond, steep stairs covered in patterned Axminster rose to the floor above.

'Is Mr Cartwright here, could you tell me, please?' Philip asked, trying to dredge from his memory what Cartwright's Christian name might be. 'Or Mrs Cartwright? Queenie?' he tried.

'Och—it's Alexander you'll be wanting,' said the woman.

Philip remembered. 'Bert,' he said.

'Bert across the border, forbye,' said the woman disparagingly. 'Alexander Herbert, he was christened. He's my brother, and he's inside now. Come away in.'

Philip followed her into the hall. When she closed the door it was quiet in the little house, away from the sound of the wind and the sea, and his ears stung from the bite of the cold air.

'I'm sorry to disturb you,' he apologized.

'Och—it's no matter,' said the woman, motioning him to continue on through the hall. She opened a door on the left, and Philip entered what must be the parlour, a small room, dimly lit, the atmosphere close and stuffy and overheated by a bright coal fire. A black upright piano stood in one corner, and a phalanx of photographs, men with sideboards and whiskers, and women in leg-of-mutton-sleeved dresses, with children in stiff white frocks or sailor suits, was arranged across a lace runner on its shining top, and continued along the dark oak overmantel above the fire. A very old woman was sitting in a high-backed chair drawn close to the blaze; her hair was white, and her face like ivory parchment wrinkled into hundreds of tiny lines. Round her shoulders she wore a crochet shawl, and there was a soft woollen rug over her knees. She had bright, beady eyes, astonishingly lively in so ancient a face, with which she looked up sharply at the newcomer.

'Why, it's Mr Philip!' From the gloomier fastnesses of the room Cartwright's familiar figure rose, astonished.

'Cartwright!' Relief filled Philip at finding his quarry had not flown.

'Sir,' Cartwright's voice was disapproving. 'You should have let us know you were coming.'

'I didn't know myself,' said Philip. 'I want your help.' He looked suddenly a little sheepish. 'It may all be a wild goose chase.' Away from Penelope and the accumulation of strange coincidences he was inclined now to blame his imagination for running away with him.

'Anything I can do, Mr Philip, of course —' said Cartwright. 'Allow me, sir, to introduce my mother.'

Philip stepped forward and shook the old lady's extended hand very gently.

'How do you do,' he said. 'I do apologize for intruding like this.'

The old woman nodded, but did not speak.

'And you've met my sister Maggie,' said Cartwright.

'Yes,' Philip said, swinging round to smile at the woman who had let him in.

'Queenie's beyond, in the kitchen, preparing the supper,' Maggie said. 'You'll stay and have a bite with us?'

Philip's taxi now blew a mournful toot on its horn to remind him that it still stood waiting out in the road.

'Your cab, that'll be, yonder,' said Cartwright. 'I'll see to him, Mr Philip.' He was gone from the room to do so before Philip could prevent him.

'And are you staying in Scotland for long?' Maggie asked in a friendly way when her brother had left the room.

'I don't know—no, not long—it depends,' said Philip vaguely, running a hand through his touselled red hair.

Maggie frowned. 'Have you only just arrived?' she asked.

'Yes—I flew in less than an hour ago,' said Philip.

'Oh—then you'll be wanting a wash,' she stated.

Philip could not know that Maggie had been a children's nanny till forced by her mother's increasing infirmity to abandon her work and come home to care for her, but he felt the effect of her professional eye.

'Er—yes, I'm afraid I'm very untidy,' he said apologetically.

In a few minutes he was upstairs meekly washing his hands and subduing his unruly hair in the bathroom. When he reappeared in the hall Cartwright had returned from paying the taxi and was carrying Philip's small valise.

'Where are you staying, Mr Philip?' he asked. 'I'll run you round later in the Ford.'

'I haven't booked in anywhere,' Philip said. 'I've never been to Edinburgh before—I'm astonished at finding you so easily—thought I might have to drive for miles.'

'How did you know we were here?' asked Cartwright. 'Are you up on a writing assignment?'

'No—I've come to see you and Queenie. Miss Prewett gave me your address,' said Philip.

At this moment Queenie emerged from the back of the house, her hair, newly washed, standing out in strong curls round her pink face, and her brown eyes alight with pleasure.

'Mr Philip!' she exclaimed, almost hugging him in her joy at seeing him. 'Oh, Mr Philip, have you seen our Penny?'

'Yes, Queenie, I have,' said Philip gravely. 'That's why I've come to see you.'

'Oh—I hope there's nothing wrong,' said Queenie. 'Tell me!'

The urgency of his mission hit Philip suddenly, afresh. They were still standing in the hall, on the point of returning to the parlour.

'I have to talk to you both,' he said. 'I'm worried.'

Queenie clasped her hands together. 'You'd best have something to eat first, Mr Philip. It's no good trying to talk on an empty stomach. I'll be patient. Bert says you've been travelling all day.'

'The flight didn't take long,' said Philip.

'I know—not like ourselves—two and a half days on the road,' said Queenie bitterly. 'But there's supper ready now—it's nothing very grand, and if you'll sit down with us we'll talk afterwards while Maggie puts Gran to bed.'

So Philip found himself sitting at the big kitchen table which was covered with a snowy cloth, eating liver and bacon with cauliflower and creamed potatoes, and talking again about America while old Mrs Cartwright presided over the meal, her knife and fork busy in her frail old hands, enjoying her food and enjoying the rare excitement of so much company and conversation, although she herself did not contribute a single word. Philip had yet to hear her utter.

After the meal she did. Before Maggie led her upstairs she said, 'Goodnight, young man,' to Philip. 'What a fine head of hair you have on you.'

Philip laughed and blushed till he threatened to clash with his hair.

'You mustn't mind Gran, Mr Philip,' said Queenie, clattering with the plates to the sink. 'She doesn't meet many strangers these days, and she was never one to mince words.'

'Oh, I don't mind,' said Philip cheerfully. He was used to being teased about the colour of his hair. 'I hope she doesn't mind me—it's an awful thing to descend on you like this so suddenly, and very good of you to give me such a wonderful meal.'

'It was nothing fancy, sir,' said Queenie. 'Just what we were having ourselves.'

'I've never met anyone yet who can cook like you,' said Philip.

Queenie beamed with pleasure. She finished stacking the dishes neatly on the draining board.

'Let's not waste more time,' she said. 'You've come all this way to see us about our Penny. It must be serious, or you'd never have come so far. Let's go into the parlour now and hear what it is.'

So they returned to the little front room. Queenie made up the fire and they sat round it, Philip, the honoured guest, in the old lady's plush-covered chair, with Cartwright and Queenie facing him in smaller chairs. He wondered what to say. Finally he asked, 'What happened? How did you really get your notice?'

'She didn't mean it, did she?' Queenie exclaimed. 'Penny'd never want us to go, anyway not without she told us herself.'

'Come, Queenie, we've had this over and over,' said Cartwright, looking uncomfortably at Philip as Queenie's eyes filled with tears and she was forced to dab at them with a spotless handkerchief. 'It was like this, Mr Philip. We had a letter from Mr Dereham saying that Miss Penelope was upset at losing her aunt, and would be selling the house as soon as she could. Meanwhile, as she would not be coming down any more to Foxbourne St Mary we were to go at the end of the week, and enclosed a month's wages.'

'Penny wouldn't do that. Penny wouldn't send us away without so much as a goodbye,' sobbed Queenie.

Cartwright grimaced at this display of emotion. He went on: 'Mr Dereham said Miss Penelope wanted to make a clean break.'

' 'Tisn't natural,' said Queenie. 'Oh, I was upset. I wanted to go and see her but Bert said not. Not if she didn't want us.'

'It's reasonable she won't want to be paying out for our wages if she's selling up,' said Cartwright, his round face looking solemn.

Philip took a deep breath. 'Penelope thinks you're still at Greyfriars,' he said. 'I'm sure she does. She'd have told me if she'd known about that letter. We'd been talking only the other day about her going down for a few days. Penny wouldn't pretend not to know if she'd sacked you.'

'Oh, no, she'd never,' Queenie said. 'She was always a truthful child.'

'She hasn't been well, and I don't think she's happy,' said Philip. 'And that doll—do you remember, the one she had at Christmas, that looked like her?'

Queenie nodded.

'It was a queer thing to give her. I don't think he did just see it in a window,' said Philip. 'I don't think Penny knew you'd had notice. He wanted you out of the way. Now why? Why should he invent a lot of nonsense?'

'He might be jealous. Jealous of her having been happy at Greyfriars,' said Queenie, pleating her damp handkerchief between her fingers.

Philip felt suddenly unable to tell these good, simple people the whole of his fears. If he was wrong, to disclose them might make it impossible for Queenie and Cartwright ever to accept Vincent if Penelope later needed and re-engaged them. If he was right, there would be time to tell them the details later when he was certain. The main thing now was to get them back to the south where he could find them easily if he wanted their help, and to discover why Vincent had sent them away from Greyfriars.

As he thought back to Christmas night something clicked into place in Philip's memory. He knew.

16

When she reached home after her visit to Betty, Penelope cleared away the breakfast dishes and tidied the house. Then she looked in Vincent's dressing-gown pocket again. The tape and the drawing pins had gone. She went slowly down the stairs, bending to peer intently at the white-painted walls. After the fourth step she found what she was looking for: small, pierced holes at either side of the fifth tread: holes that could have been made by drawing pins.

She stood up again. So he had meant her to fall down the stairs. Why did he want to harm her? Such a short fall would be most unlikely to kill her. He must be insane. Perhaps he merely wanted her out of the way, to free him. But she had been inactive for over a week, ailing and sick. If he meant to hurt her why was he so kind about bringing her supper in bed and drinks of hot milk? Was it his bad conscience? Her mind ran about like a rat in a trap. She went back to the bedroom and picked up the doll. Whatever he had meant when he gave it to her, it could not harm her now; surely he had not intended that it should? Finding a doll that looked like she did was a coincidence, that was all.

She remembered again her fall from the step of the bus, and the busy helpfulness of the unknown blonde woman with the umbrella. Why exactly had she fallen? Why had the women been so close behind? And how had she scratched the beak handle of her umbrella? If she had purposely tripped Penelope with it, how had she known she would be on that bus? Another coincidence.

Or was it? Penelope, with a sinking heart, remembered Vincent asking her the day before what were her plans. If the woman knew what she looked like, which she could easily have discovered from a photograph, it would be simple to follow her from the dentist's consulting rooms and wait for an opportunity. Perhaps she had hoped to follow her into the Underground and push her in front of a train. Penelope shuddered. Why?

She took a grip on herself. She must know more. She wrapped the doll up in some tissue paper and set forth for the King's Road. Up and down the length of it she went, into every possible shop to ask if they had recently sold this and a similar doll to anyone, possibly a tall fair man with a small moustache, or a blonde woman in her thirties. But none of the shops stocked any dolls remotely like hers; virtually none were made of china; their bodies and faces were of various plastics. In one the old man behind the counter told her the doll she carried was probably German, and pointed out that its clothes were hand-made.

It was clear by the end of the afternoon that the doll had not been bought in Chelsea. Penelope went home again and put it prominently on the sitting-room mantelpiece.

When Vincent returned at half-past seven—earlier than usual—she had changed into her green velvet dress, and pinned the diamond brooch to her shoulder. Her face was slightly flushed, and her eyes, large-pupilled, shone with nervous excitement.

'How smart we are tonight, sweetheart,' said Vincent in surprise, crossing the room to hold her by the shoulders. She swung away from him before he could kiss her.

'Sherry?' she asked, going to the decanter which she had put on a table in the corner.

'Thank you.'

'I'm feeling lots better,' Penelope said, pouring him out a glass. Her hand was perfectly steady as she gave it to him. 'So I thought it was time I dressed up and that we might celebrate. We've been married four months today, you know. Or are you too tired to go out?'

Here was his chance to say no, but he was too broke because he had lost his job.

'Good idea,' Vincent said. 'Where shall we go?'

'Let's go to Bellini's,' said Penelope. This was somewhere they had visited often during the weeks before they married.

'Right,' Vincent said. 'I'll give them a ring to book a table and go and change. Give me a minute. 'Whistling, he went upstairs, carrying his sherry glass, refilled. Penelope dranks hers at a gulp. She felt she needed courage of whatever sort.

'Phew,' she said to herself, peering at her reflection in the mirror which was fixed to the wall facing the door. Her heart was thudding hard, and her hands were damp. She took several deep breaths to calm herself. When Vincent returned she was sitting composedly in her chair apparently reading the latest copy of *Vogue.*

She chattered gaily during dinner. Vincent looked at her speculatively once or twice; she thought he must be wondering at her rapid recovery. They discussed the other people in the restaurant, the possibility of an Italian holiday later in the year, and winter sports. It was the sort of conversation they had exchanged during the brief weeks between their first meeting and their engagement, but now Penelope felt exactly as if she were acting in a play and might forget her part. She had not time to allow the thought that Vincent, this man, her husband, was a stranger about whom she knew almost nothing; she had no time now for fear; she was fully occupied avoiding a silence. After a while she began to think she might be dreaming, and might even have dreamed about the china doll, the piece of tape, and the woman. She found herself alternating between an inability to look Vincent squarely in the face, and a desire to stare at him intently in an endeavour to solve the puzzle, wondering if she was broken-hearted or simply frightened, and which was worse.

They danced for a while, and there was then no need to talk, but to her horror Penelope found that she could hardly bring herself to touch him. The feel of his arms about her, which once had been enough to make her experience a surge of delight, now made her want to shrink away from him. She made some excuse about still feeling weak, and they left the floor. As they did so, they brushed against another couple, and the woman, turning to see who had knocked into her, said: 'Why hullo! How's the little girl?'

Vincent stared at her. His face remained impassive. She was a very tall girl, with ash-blonde hair and wearing a heavy armour of make-up. He made no reply but merely propelled Penelope back to their table.

'Who was that?' she asked. 'What little girl did she mean?'

'I've no idea,' said Vincent coolly. 'She must have mistaken me for someone else.'

Penelope wondered whether to believe him. This was not the umbrella one; this was a much younger, smarter type. She was not really surprised when in a few minutes

Vincent suggested that she must not get over-tired and perhaps they had better leave.

He was cheerful in the car going home; he drove fast, jumping the lights and showing off. When they reached the house he went at once to pour himself out a whisky and soda, and then crossed to the mantelpiece in the sitting-room where the doll sat.

'I see you've found a new place for her,' he said.

'Yes—I thought she looked nice there,' Penelope said lightly, throwing her coat down on a chair.

'How like you she is,' Vincent said, holding the doll in his left hand.

'Yes,' she agreed. 'Where did you say you found her?'

'In the King's Road,' he said idly. He put the doll down again and came towards Penelope. She moved away and began fiddling with her coat, pretending to look for a handkerchief.

'Did you have a good day at work?' she asked, her back turned to him. She swung round to watch him while he answered.

'Oh yes,' he said. 'Sold a ten-thousand pound car to an oil sheikh.'

She took a breath. 'Were you in the office all day?'

'Yes—except for when I took him out for a spin this afternoon,' Vincent said.

'Oh,' she replied. 'I'm glad you had good luck.'

'Why so curious?' he asked.

'You never talk about your work. I wish you would,' she said. 'I'd like to know about it.' What would happen if she faced him squarely and said she knew he had not been near Automobile Kings? Why was he so sure she did not know? He must have great confidence in her obedience. She wished she had the courage to challenge him. 'I went to see Betty,' she said, instead.

'Oh—that was nice, dear,' he said. 'I'm glad.' He stood, very large, by the white-painted fireplace, looking down at her.

'I am a bit tired,' she said now. 'Thank you for the nice evening, Vincent. I'm going to bed.'

She picked up her coat and hurried from the room. Left alone, Vincent poured himself out another drink. He looked at the doll again, picked it up and turned it round in his strong hand. Presently he followed Penelope upstairs.

She seemed to be asleep, her back turned to him and only the top of her head visible above the sheet. Vincent looked down at her for a moment, and her heart thumped as she tried to breathe evenly. After a few seconds he turned away and she heard him moving quietly about the room. She did not relax until she knew by his slight snores that he slept.

In the morning she caught an early train to Hampshire. When she arrived at the nearest station to Foxbourne St. Mary she went straight to the telephone box on platform one and rang up the Torringtons. She had to talk to someone, and Philip was the one person to whom she knew she could tell the whole story; he would neither ridicule her nor falsely console her.

The voice of the Torringtons' daily help answered. Penelope pressed button A and asked for Philip.

'I'm sorry, miss. Mr Philip's gone to Scotland,' she was told. 'Don't know when he'll be back, I'm sure. He didn't say.'

Penelope replaced the receiver without answering. She felt utterly stricken and forlorn. There was no reason why

Philip shouldn't go to Scotland; but she had never thought of such a thing: she had expected him to be at home, able to help her. Scotland! It might as well be Timbuctoo: both seemed equally inaccessible. How silly not to have telephoned him first before leaving London. Now her whole journey was in vain. She looked at her watch; it was a quarter past twelve. She could go out to Greyfriars: Queenie would help: Queenie would listen.

She took a taxi. She seemed to have been in a lot of taxis lately. She paid it off before going to the front door of the house. It took her a quarter of an hour to convince herself that the house was empty, and she could not get into it because she had no key.

When Penelope walked up the village street a few minutes later there was no one about. Miss Prewett's post office was closed for the lunch hour; her tabby cat was crouched on the top of the gatepost solemnly staring into space with a meditative look on its face. Outside Major Tompkins' house the spaniel was rootling in the ditch; he wagged his tail as Penelope went by, and she paused to pat his head and rub him behind the ears. She went on to the cottage further along the lane where Kitty Francis lived with her loom and her potter's wheel.

Kitty was eating her frugal lunch on a corner of the kitchen table, with *The Daily Telegraph* propped against a loaf of bread in front of her, when Penelope knocked at the door. She was startled to see who her visitor was, and fussed about her, bustling her in to get warm.

'Have you had lunch?' Kitty asked, and when Penelope shook her head she said, 'Well, come along my dear. I'll soon find you something.'

Penelope was led into the small, cheerful kitchen. She was weary again beyond measure, and glad to sit down and wait meekly, without talking, while a bowl of soup was prepared and thin slices of roast beef cut from the joint Kitty had cooked when Major Tompkins came to lunch two days before. She was surprised to find that she was very hungry, and that she was able to eat. She managed an apple after the beef, one of the Major's Cox's which he stored and shared with Kitty in the winter.

Afterwards Kitty took her into the studio. This was a large room occupying most of the ground floor of the cottage. At one end was the wheel and the loom; and in the middle an efficient slow-combustion stove kept the room thoroughly warm however cold the weather grew outside. Kitty opened its doors and poked it, then added a couple of logs to the fire inside. Penelope sat down on the sofa and leaned her head back against the cushions while Kitty moved about pulling up another chair and pushing the cat off a third. She closed her eyes. When Kitty turned round again she saw that her visitor slept.

Life had not always been kind to Kitty. By being something of an eccentric she achieved a sort of confidence; but she had not forgotten what it was like to be *in extremis*. She had recognized despair in Penelope's eyes when she had opened the door, and deliberately delayed her from disclosing the trouble; misfortunes described are misfortunes acknowledged. Sometimes, left unrevealed, they can be surmounted. If Penelope still wanted to talk after her lunch then Kitty was ready to be her confidante and help her if she could. Now, looking at the slight figure stretched out on the sofa, she felt a pang of envy for the power of youth so easily to pull down the blind. She found a rug, hand woven by herself, and gently draped it over the girl. Then she sat down by the fire to wait, wondering just exactly what the trouble was, and why it was she who had been chosen to hear about it.

Penelope slept till half-past four. When she woke the room was nearly dark, lit by the flickering glow of the fire. It took her a few minutes to remember where she was and what had happened: Philip was in Scotland, Greyfriars deserted; and she was at Kitty's cottage.

'Queenie and Cartwright! They've gone!' she said. 'Where are they?' She sat up, rubbing her eyes.

'You gave them notice, my dear,' Kitty said. 'Had you forgotten?' She got up and switched on a tall lamp with a painted shade which stood in a corner of the room.

'No, no I didn't!' Penelope said.

'But you did, dear. They were very upset,' said Kitty, with reproof in her voice.

'I didn't,' Penelope insisted, swinging her legs to the floor. 'I don't know what you mean.'

Kitty explained then, repeating the story which Major Tompkins had told Philip.

'But I didn't say that—I never did,' Penelope almost shouted. 'I never asked Vincent to sack them.'

'Perhaps he thought it was better for you to do it like this,' said Kitty soothingly. 'After all, you'll be selling Greyfriars, won't you?'

'I don't know—I hadn't thought about it yet,' said Penelope. 'He shouldn't have done it without telling me.' She looked distraught, so that Kitty felt some sympathy for Vincent even if she disagreed with what he had done. Penelope looked now at her watch. 'Heavens, look at the time,' she said. 'I'll never get back to London now before he does.'

'Surely that doesn't matter?' said Kitty.

'Oh yes it does—he mustn't know I'm here,' said Penelope. She looked terrified.

'Well, if you can't get back in time you'll have to tell him,' said Kitty. She looked intently at her guest. 'You seem very tired, Penny dear. Wouldn't you like to stay the night? You could ring up.'

'Could you have me?' Penelope asked.

'Of course, my dear. I can lend you a nightdress, and I always keep a spare new toothbrush just in case,' said Kitty.

Penelope was warm and safe. She longed to stay.

'I think it could be managed,' she said thoughtfully, remembering Betty. 'I know what to do now.'

17

The vauxhall was still warm. Vincent, after Betty's telephone call, ran down the stairs of the little house, opened the front door and went out into the night once more. He moved with surprising lightness for such a big man, and was soon back in the driver's seat of his car. The engine started almost without a sound: he slipped the clutch in, and drove smoothly away from the kerb, down the narrow mews road to the wide street at the end, and turned to the right. It was foggy again, but the fog was not thick enough to prove a menace. The street lights shining through the dense air wore the effect of blurred haloes round them. Vincent hummed a tune under his breath as he picked his way along in and out of the evening traffic towards Soho. He had been surprised to learn that Penelope was staying the night with Betty; but he quickly accepted the situation and was not one to waste an unexpected opportunity.

He parked the car in a quiet side street and locked it. Then he walked along the pavement for some fifty yards till he reached a basement stairway, down which he went. A yellow-painted door admitted him, at the bottom, into a restaurant. It was small, with closely-packed tables arranged in crowded intimacy round a stamp-sized dance floor. A three-piece band on a small raised dais at one end was playing skiffle—three lads with pallid faces, flopping hair and wearing loose, brightly-checked shirts and jeans. Speechless couples vibrated round on the tiny space available; the air was hazy with the smoke of many cigarettes, and very gloomy, illumined only by a few bulbs concealed behind trailing foliage high on the walls.

Vincent made his way past the entranced couples to an empty table in a corner and sat down, nodding at the three members of the band as he passed their platform. One of them, still twanging his guitar, rose and went off the stage through a slit in the shabby black velvet curtain that made a backdrop. He reappeared almost at once, and was soon followed by the tall, blonde woman whom Penelope had seen with Vincent at Sycamore Gardens the day before. Tonight she wore a short evening dress, full-skirted black tulle mounted over pink, with a tight strapless bodice picked out in black sequins. She crossed behind the band and came to join Vincent at his table.

'What have you done with the little woman?' she asked, sitting down.

Vincent grinned. 'She's left me,' he said.

'Oh—not really?' Mock display appeared on the well-made-up features.

He shook his head. 'Not to worry. Sleeping with a school friend,' he said. 'Her nerves are in a jangle and she has a headache.'

The woman smiled. She was handsome, in a generous way, with high colouring that was not all artificial, and very white teeth. The skin of her arms and shoulders looked warm and velvety. She had plump hands with dimpled knuckles, and wore no rings.

'This calls for a celebration,' she said. 'Your first night off the lead.' She turned and beckoned to the gloom surrounding them. Through it appeared a flat-footed waiter who seemed to be of Asiatic origin. She spoke to him authoritatively, and then turned again to face Vincent.

'Quite like old times,' she said.

Vincent nodded. 'Just you wait—this is nothing,' he said.

'I'll take the evening off,' she said softly, 'after we've had dinner.'

The waiter returned then, bringing champagne on ice in a bucket, and there was a few minutes' close concentration while the meal was chosen. Then Vincent and his companion relaxed.

During the dinner that followed the woman left their table to sing a couple of sentimental songs with the band. She had good voice, low-pitched, and some skill; there was a professional manner about her delivery that was wasted on her present audience.

'I'd forgotten how good you were, Clarrie,' said Vincent, still applauding as she returned to him after her performance.

'It bores me now,' she said.

They left the restaurant soon afterwards and walked down the road to the Vauxhall. They were almost of a height, a striking couple, both fair-haired and confident.

'Take me home,' Clarrie commanded when they were in the car. 'Back to your place.'

'No, Clarrie. You know we agreed it was too risky,' he protested.

'She's away—it's quite safe,' said Clarrie. 'I'm curious to see the love nest.'

Vincent chuckled. 'The neighbours might see you, he said.

'They'll think I'm potty Penelope,' she said. 'I'll shrink and look clinging.'

'As if you could,' he laughed. 'Oh, very well. I don't suppose anyone will see you in the fog.'

So it was that some twenty minutes later Clarrie entered the little mews house and stood giggling in the hall. Hanging on Vincent's arm she insisted on making a grand tour of the place.

'Very genteel, I must say,' she commented. 'Absolutely U.' She picked up one of Penelope's silver-backed, monogrammed hairbrushes and inspected it. Then she peered in the wardrobe and examined Penelope's clothes.

'Hm. Very teenage,' she said, extracting a pale blue woollen dress on a hanger and waving it in the air. She put it back, and pulled out a fold of green velvet. 'I know this one,' she said with a chuckle. She bent and looked at the shoes arranged below. 'What small feet you've got my dear,' she intoned in a deep voice.

'Put them back, Clarrie,' Vincent urged. 'She'll see someone's been at them.'

'Well, you don't mind that, do you? Tell her she did it herself when she was sleep-walking,' said Clarrie, but she put the shoes down and closed the cupboard. 'Not to my taste at all, all this walnut and brocade,' she said. 'I prefer contemporary myself.' She paused in front of Penelope's long mirror to admire her reflection as she said this, and Vincent, from behind, put his arms round her.

After a time she detached herself from his embrace.

'How much longer will it take?' she asked.

Vincent took her arm and they began to go downstairs to the sitting-room.

'Not long,' he said. 'She was out for hours in the fog the other day—she came back soaking wet, and she'd forgotten the key and shut herself out. I told you, she's simple.'

'Poor kid—in a way I can't help feeling sorry for her,' said Clarrie, crossing to the mantelpiece and picking up the doll. 'Funny—I never really thought it would work, just an idea in her mind, sort of.'

'No one will miss her,' said Vincent. 'The world's better off without her sort. She's not worth a tear. It's people like you, Clarrie, who count.'

'And I know who'd miss me,' said Clarrie, turning to face him, the full skirts of her dress swirling round her as she moved. 'When do I get my brooch back?'

He frowned. 'Oh—as soon as it's over, of course,' he said. 'Not long now.'

'Let me have it. Please! I miss it,' Clarrie said. 'Look how bare this dress is without it. I bet the silly bit never wears it—probably thinks it's too good.'

'Oh, she does,' said Vincent. 'She wore it last night. I took her out on the town—thought I'd better, she wanted to. Funny thing—ran into that girl from the shop where the doll came from.' He frowned. 'She was dancing. Recognized me.'

'Did the kid notice?'

'Not to matter. I made out it was a mistake,' said Vincent. He tapped a finger against his teeth, thoughtfully, looking at Clarrie. Then he moved towards her. 'God, it's good to see you. You shall have your brooch tonight. The kid'll think she's lost it, and it'll be just another nail in her coffin. Ha! That's good, another nail in her coffin!'

He was still laughing when his mouth closed down hard on Clarrie's.

18

It was early afternoon when Philip flew in to London Airport again after his swift visit to Edinburgh. Queenie was with him. Philip collected his car from the big open parking space and she got into it beside him. He drove her to Waterloo where she was to catch a train down to Hampshire. Then he roared off in the direction of Kensington.

There was no answer when he rang the front-door bell at the little house in the mews. Philip looked at his watch. It was three o'clock. Penelope must be out shopping, at least he hoped that was the reason she did not appear. He walked slowly up the narrow road to the corner where it joined the wider street, by the house with the shabby railings and the tall, gaunt tree. He looked up the street to see if she was in sight, returning, but he could not recognize her among the people that he saw walking along the pavement. He stood for a moment, rocking to and fro on his heels, staring at the tree reflectively. A few dried husks, the shrivelled pods of the seeds, clung to the black branches. Idly Philip pulled a handful from the tree and rubbed them in his hand. The paper-like husks revealed small black seeds. He pocketed them, absently, and then walked slowly back again to the house, his red hair a bright blob in the otherwise drab winter scene where already the beginnings of fog were rising. He tried Penelope's bell once again, but when no one answered he got into his car and drove away.

He parked down a turning off the King's Road, and began a tour of the shops in the area. Like Penelope the day before, he went into every one that might possibly have stocked the doll Vincent had given her.

An old, bald man with rimless spectacles who was the owner of one shop peered at him with interest.

'How unusual,' he said. 'I had a young lady in here only yesterday with a doll very much like the one you describe. She wanted to know if it had been bought here.'

'Oh? What sort of young lady? Small, and dark?' Philip asked, his ginger eyebrows shooting up in anxious enquiry.

'Yes, indeed. Very young—about eighteen. Pale and thin,' said the old man, waving his hands about in a gesture to indicate height and size. 'Blue eyes.'

'I see.' Philip thought for a moment. 'Well, thanks,' he said at last.

'I told her the doll had probably been made in Germany,' volunteered the old man. 'It was china, and its clothes were all hand made. She's a friend of yours, I expect, sir?'

'Yes—yes she is,' said Philip. 'Well, thanks very much,' he repeated and hurried out of the shop.

So Penelope had been making enquiries about the doll: that meant something must have made her suspicious. What could have happened in the last few days to make her suspect that Vincent had lied to her? He hastened along the road to the nearest telephone box and dialled the number of her house. The ringing tone came back to him, blank, discouraging, defeating. At last he replaced his own receiver and went out into the road again to continue the search for a shop that might have sold the doll, but now he asked also if anyone else had made similar enquiries lately. Three more shops confirmed that a girl had brought in a doll, such as he described, the day before.

Philip returned to his car and drove back to the mews. It was nearly dark now, and the street lights were on, but there was no light in any window of the house where Penelope lived. He rang the bell: then, when there was no answer, he took a bunch of keys out of his pocket and began trying them one by one in the door, hoping that no one was watching his extraordinary behaviour. Before returning from Edinburgh that morning he had gone with Cartwright to visit a useful friend who lived in an obscure part of the city, and was known by Cartwright to possess a number of varied and unusual instruments, and to be a fund of information about a great many things that were not strictly conventional. Thanks to this friend Philip, after a few false starts, found that the door was responding.

He was soon inside. He slipped his shoes off in the hall, in case they marked the thick new carpets that covered the floors, and stuffed them into the pockets of his raincoat as he went upstairs. He had very soon explored the house and made sure that it was empty. There was pathos in thus spying inquisitively upon Penelope's life, but Philip did not waste time in thinking of this. He went round every inch of the house. He noticed the doll in its new place on the sitting-room mantelpiece; he went upstairs, looked in Penelope's jewel case in a drawer of her dressing-table and saw her diamond brooch: the stones were real, that was certain. He went into the bathroom, bare and tidy with just the towels that hung on the rail and the plastic tooth-mug sitting in a chromium ring plugged to the wall. Toothbrushes and paste were out of sight, kept in the cupboard, he remembered, beside the Elastoplast and Dettol. Penelope's pink-flowered bath cap hung on a hook behind the door.

He went downstairs to the kitchen and glanced around. He saw the green tin tea-caddy standing on a shelf beside the cooker. It had been empty the day that he had come to tea, when Penelope was sick. He lifted the lid and looked inside. It was half full. He found some newspaper in a drawer and tore off a sheet of *The Daily Mail,* which he put on the table. Then, very carefully, he emptied the tea out of the caddy on to the paper. Next, he searched in his pocket and took out an old envelope. Into it he put the last leaves that remained in the tin. Slowly he returned the rest of the tea into it again. It made a small, dusty commotion in the air as it settled. Philip closed the tin and replaced it on the shelf. Then he pocketed the piece of newspaper. He went downstairs, put his shoes on again in the hall, and let himself quietly out of the house. There was still no sign of Penelope. He went back to his car and sat in it for a time, waiting, sure that she must return soon, his fingers drumming on the steering wheel. At last he gave up, started the engine and drove away. It would not be a good thing if Vincent returned and found him there: explanations might at this stage be difficult.

He drove about rather aimlessly for a time. Then he telephoned the house in the mews again. Still there was no answer. It was late now; the shops had shut, and Penelope should be coming home, if she was the dutiful wife he imagined her to be, to wait for the return of Vincent from his labours. Philip found himself driving slowly along Bond Street. He turned off, up a side road; the traffic was thick now with the onset of the rush hour and he felt he had been foolish to come so far west. People were scurrying along the pavements in the half haze of the slight fog, and the buses had multiplied, coming in droves along the road. He pulled out to keep in the centre stream of traffic, and as he did so a black police car swooped past and drew up a short distance ahead. Philip had to concentrate on the immediate problem of making his own car proceed in obedience to the signals of a constable who had sprung up like a mushroom to direct the traffic past an obstruction in the road. Philip noticed an ambulance, white and ghostly in the gloom, and as he went past he realized that whatever the accident was which had caused all the confusion, it had happened close to the shop where Vincent and he had bought their dolls.

Farther down the road there was a space to park by the kerb. On impulse Philip drew in and pulled up. He walked back up the road to the scene of the accident. The crowd that was gathering was being dispersed by the police. Barriers were going up to fence off the pavement outside the shop. The ambulance waited, and the bystanders, disappointed, moved grumbingly away. Philip saw two bustling men in plain clothes come out of the shop, look up and down the road, confer with each other and then enter the shop again. He could see them moving, dark and bulky against the brightly-lit interior of the shop.

'What's up?' he asked a man walking past in the crowd. 'Someone run over?'

'No—someone in the shop copped it—that's a C.I.D. car,' said his informant, glad to be knowledgeable.

'What—killed? An accident?' Philip felt the hairs on the back of his neck prickling with horror. 'Or what?'

'I should say not an accident—be in the evening papers, I expect,' said the man cheerfully. 'They won't let you get near, mate.'

Philip stared at him. 'I suppose not,' he said.

'Never know when it's got your number on it, do you?' said the man blithely. 'I always say if you're for it, you're for it—take your life in your hands every time you cross the road, don't you?'

Philip agreed, and the man went walking off down the street, whistling.

Philip went up to one of the policemen standing outside the shop.

'What's up?' he asked.

'Never you mind, sir—pass along please,' said the constable sternly.

It was useless to persist, Philip saw. He knew well enough that the police did not hand out information till they were ready. A cluster of newspaper reporters at the other end of the pavement was also getting short shrift so it was no good producing his Press card. He brushed past the barrier and joined them. Two of them were men he knew slightly, and after greeting them he asked them what was the cause of all the excitement.

'Some girl who works in that place got knifed,' he was told. 'Chap went in to buy a flower vase or something and found her. The police won't give us anything on it yet.'

'Who did it? Was it robbery?' asked Philip.

'Haven't a clue—might be sex,' said the reporter hopefully. 'She was an attractive piece, I believe.'

Philip turned away. So she was dead, that tall, appealing creature with all the eye-shadow. Someone had come into the shop and stabbed her—a madman, a thief, a lover—who? But Philip knew. He walked slowly back to his car; in his pocket the envelope with the grains of tea rustled as he moved.

19

There was still no reply from Penelope's number when Philip telephoned again. He drove slowly back to Kensington, parked his car two hundred yards from the turning to the mews, and went the rest of the way on foot. At the corner he paused, beneath the branches of the shadowy tree, as a car changed gear and turned down the narrow road beside him. It was a Vauxhall. Philip strode down the mews behind it, and was in time to see the lights go on in the little house after Vincent entered. For a moment the figure of the other man was visible, illumined at the first-floor window, before he drew the curtains. Philip remained outside, withdrawn into the shelter of the warehouse doorway opposite, waiting for Penelope to come home, but she did not appear; it was Vincent who left the house again, almost an hour later.

Philip tried to control his alarm. He was sure that Penelope would not be in the habit of staying out all day until so late. She must have gone to spend the day with a friend, or be staying away; or else something very unusual must have happened to detain her. He was convinced that she would take her housewifely duties very seriously and always be at home when Vincent got back from work unless prevented by something unforeseen. He could not believe that he was too late already.

He went away to the telephone box nearby and rang up Queenie who was now back in Foxbourne St. Mary. She was not at Greyfriars but at The Feathers, where her father was still landlord.

'Queenie, do you know of any friend of Penelope's where she might go to spend the day?' he asked, when she answered. 'She isn't at home. I'm worried.'

'Well, now, let me see, Mr Philip.' Queenie's voice came to him with maddening slowness. 'There's quite a few of her school friends living in London. Let's think.' She hesitated, and then told him a few names, but could furnish no addresses. Philip wrote them all down.

'Of course, some of these young ladies are married now,' Queenie added. 'That Betty—now what's her name? She and Penny were great chums. Marlborough, was it? Some town, I know. Oh—Swindon, that was it.'

'Thanks, Queenie,' said Philip. 'I expect she's at an Old Girls' party or something, but I do feel a bit anxious.'

'There's no one belonging to her who knows where she is,' said Queenie. 'It's not right, Mr Philip.'

'Only Dereham,' said Philip grimly. He thought that Penelope had only Vincent who did belong to her, and the value of that condition was questionable.

'Ring us again, Mr Philip, when you find her,' begged Queenie, now as apprehensive as he was himself.

Philip promised to do so, although he was doubtful if his search had any hope of success. He was beginning to feel desperately afraid. He looked at the short list of names which he had scribbled on an old envelope. This Betty one sounded the most likely, so he decided to try her first. There were a great many Swindons in the telephone directory, and it took him a long time and a great many fourpences before he found a Mrs Swindon who owned the name of Betty.

'You are the Mrs Swindon who is a friend of Penelope—Dereham?' Philip hesitated over the still unfamiliar surname.

The strange voice became instantly guarded as it admitted the connection.

'I suppose you don't happen to know where she is at present, do you?' Philip asked. 'Has she been to see you today? It's Philip Torrington speaking, I'm a friend of Penny's.'

'Oh.' The voice sounded doubtful. 'Well—yes—I say, is everything all right?'

'I don't know,' Philip said. 'That's what I'm trying to find out. I don't know where Penelope is.'

'Oh. Well, she's perfectly safe, she's staying here for the night,' said the voice firmly.

'Is she? Oh, thank goodness!' There was vast relief in Philip's voice. 'Can I speak to her?'

'Oh no—no, I'm afraid that's impossible,' said Betty. 'She's got a headache and gone to bed early.'

'I see,' Philip said. 'Well, thank you. I'm sorry to disturb you.'

After he had replaced the receiver he stood in the box for a few minutes, thinking, thankfulness his chief reaction. Then he rang up Queenie to say Penelope had been located. But his mind was still far from easy. Mrs Swindon had seemed disconcerted by his enquiry. She had anxiously asked if everything was all right, as though she too expected it not to be. Perhaps Penelope was ill again.

He swung out of the box and hurried back to his car. In a few minutes he was standing on yet another doorstep ringing the bell, this time that of Derek and Betty Swindon. Bolts were drawn on the other side of the door, and then it was opened by a thickset young man a few years older than Philip. He stared suspiciously at the caller.

'I'm Philip Torrington—I rang up ten minutes ago about Penelope—Mrs Swindon said she was staying here,' he said.

Derek Swindon frowned. 'I'm afraid you can't see her,' he said firmly.

'She isn't really ill, is she?' asked Philip. 'Is she all right?'

'She's quite all right,' Derek said, looking as if he was about to close the front door in Philip's face. But he was prevented: a young woman came out into the narrow hall of the house from one of the ground-floor rooms. She spoke directly to Philip.

'I think you'd better come in,' she said. 'Derek, let him in. He's a friend of Penny's.'

Somewhat reluctantly Derek stood aside to let Philip enter the house. Betty came forward and shook hands with him.

'We spoke on the telephone—please come in,' she said, and led the way into the sitting-room which overlooked the road, a long, narrow room the width of the house, comfortably furnished, and with a bright coal fire burning.

'Do sit down,' said Betty, waving him to a linen-covered chair at one side of the fireplace.

Philip obeyed. His red hair was untidy and his face looked anxious. Derek, with disapproval radiating from him, went to the far end of the room where a carved corner cupboard held bottles and glasses.

'Whisky?' he offered.

'Thanks,' said Philip, who needed it. 'Now, about Penny.'

'Yes,' said Betty. 'About Penny.' She had been subjecting Philip to an intensive scrutiny during the short interval in which he had been in her house. 'I remember hearing Penny talk about you—you've known her for years, haven't you? I'm sorry if I was rude on the telephone—I thought you might be that Vincent in disguise, trying to find out where she really is.'

'But isn't she here?' asked Philip, springing to his feet at once.

'Betty, do be careful,' said Derek, returning with Philip's drink which he placed beside him on a small table. 'I don't like this business.'

'I don't either,' said Betty. 'That's why we must talk to him—he's worried and so are we.'

'For God's sake tell me where Penny is,' Philip almost shouted.

'Calm down,' said Derek. 'She's staying with some old girl in the country—she rang up to ask Betty to say she was here. For some reason she didn't want her husband to know where she really was.'

'She's perfectly safe,' Betty added. 'She rang up at about half-past four.'

'Thank heaven,' Philip muttered, taking a large swallow of his whisky and soda.

'Why are you so concerned about her?' Betty asked then.

'I don't like her husband,' said Philip flatly.

'She's not a bit happy,' said Betty. She hesitated, glancing doubtfully at Derek.

'Betty's been worried about Penelope for some time,' said Derek, abruptly relinquishing his hostile manner. 'Thought she seemed to be getting into a bad state of nerves—she came round a few days ago. I think you'd better tell him, darling. If he can help it's justified. He's met Vincent and we haven't.'

'We couldn't go to the wedding because I was having Stephen,' Betty explained. 'And anyway it all seemed rather rushed. I will tell you as much as I know.' She paused, collecting her thoughts to decide where to begin. 'I hadn't seen Penny since she was married until she came to lunch a few weeks ago, not very long after her aunt died,' she said. 'I hardly recognized her—she was so thin, and jumpy. She'd fallen off a bus on her way here, and then nearly got herself run over just outside.' She went on to tell Philip all that she knew, ending with Penelope's fleeting visit two days before and her disclosure about the blonde woman in Vincent's car.

'I see.' Philip's face was hard. He had listened in silence to the story. 'I'd heard about the accidents—the bus and the black Humber. I hadn't heard about the woman.'

'Do you think there's anything in it?' Derek asked. 'It could have a hundred innocent explanations.'

'Of course it could, but I'm sure it hasn't,' said Philip definitely. 'I've had a horrible hunch about all this for ages. Dereham isn't the sort of chap to fall for a girl like Penelope—doubt if he could fall for anyone, really, if you know what I mean.' He frowned. 'He gave her a doll for Christmas. It looked just like her. It was a very queer thing to do.'

'I thought he gave her a diamond brooch,' said Betty.

'Yes, he gave her that as well,' said Philip. 'A beauty.'

'Sounds as if he was fond of her all right,' suggested Derek.

'Conscience,' said Betty.

Philip hesitated. 'I've got a theory,' he said. 'You'll think I'm quite mad, I'm sure. I've no proof—it's all guesswork and hunches.'

'We'll listen,' said Betty. 'Go on, Philip—I can't call you Mr Torrington. I'm worried to death about Penny she's miserable and wretched and she should never have married that man. Why did she?'

'Yes, why did she?' repeated Philip. 'That's the key — that's the foundation on sand. He must have flattered her—she's not very old and not very experienced, and he's good-looking, I suppose, in a smooth sort of way—you've seen photographs, I expect—rather like a stage Guards officer.'

'Yes, he is like that,' Betty agreed. 'I saw some wedding photographs.'

'I think he married her because he knew she would inherit a considerable fortune one day,' said Philip. 'If he made up his mind to sweep her off her feet it wouldn't be very difficult.'

'But he's got—he had—a very good job—he's a company director, or something,' protested Betty. 'He didn't need money.'

'He might like being idle—lots of people do,' said Philip. 'None of us seems to know much about him before he married Penny. I asked the old boy who introduced them and it turned out he really scarcely knew Dereham at all, though everyone thought they were old friends.' He looked at both his listeners. 'I think it's worse than just marrying her for her money,' he said slowly. 'I think he wants to kill her, or make her kill herself?'

If he had expected to startle them he certainly succeeded. Both his listeners stared at him open-mouthed.

Philip went on: 'I think he meant her to get the idea that she was doomed. He gave her that doll, which looks like her, and when it got broken he replaced it. Then at dinner on Christmas night at Foxbourne St. Mary there was a lot of talk about voodoo and waxen images and so forth, and someone told a story about a superstitious African who died of fright, sort of auto-suggestion, because he'd been cursed. It was Dereham who made the other fellow tell the story.

'Then Penelope had various accidents—she fell off the bus and was nearly run over, and you say she fell down the stairs. And she's been sick.'

'But Vincent couldn't have pushed her off the bus, or down the stairs—she'd have seen him,' protested Betty.

'No. But he could have tried to run over her. There is a big black secondhand Humber for sale at Automobile Kings, where Dereham works,' said Philip. He told them about his visit to the showrooms, and then he described Penelope's sickness and the unlikely dismissal of the Cartwrights.

'But murder—you can't be right!' said Derek.

'I don't think he meant to kill her with his own hands,' said Philip, now striding up and down before the fire. 'It's more subtle. He intended her to have some frightening accidents which would make her think the dice were loaded against her. If there were enough, and if she lost a lot of sleep and was afraid and miserable, she might believe that she was doomed. He could have intended to work her up into such a nervous state that she would do it herself.'

'Oh God! Oh, Derek, do you really think she's all right tonight?' exclaimed Betty. 'That Vincent might have made her do the telephoning as a blind, though he sounded surprised enough when I spoke to him. He's not working at Automobile Kings any more, by the way.' She quickly related what Penelope had told her about that other telephone call.

'You said she sounded cheerful,' Derek pointed out. 'She must be all right.'

'She's with a Miss Francis, in Foxbourne St. Mary,' said Betty, now nearly in tears.

'Well, we can soon find out,' said Philip firmly. 'May I use your phone?'

'Of course,' replied Derek and Betty in unison.

While he waited for the exchange to get Kitty Francis' number, Philip explained that she was an art-and-craft exponent whom Penelope had known for years. Soon he was speaking directly to her, and as they listened to the short, one-sided conversation, Betty and Derek visibly began to relax when they saw the tension begin to leave Philip as he smiled and rubbed his free hand through his untidy hair in relief.

'Well, she is there all right,' he said, when he had replaced the receiver. 'Old Kitty said she was in a bit of a state, and very tired. She's asleep. She didn't know about Greyfriars and the Cartwrights, of course; Kitty said she had no difficulty in persuading her to stay the night once she'd thought of ringing you and fixing the story for Vincent. She doesn't know quite why she came to Foxbourne, though. Do you?'

'No,' said Betty. 'She obviously didn't want to say much. She said she'd explain later.'

'Well, we've got a breathing space now, anyway,' said Philip. 'Time to make a plan.' He turned his back on them both for a moment, and they exchanged a glance, while he gazed into the fire. Then he turned and addressed them.

'I don't think Dereham means to do anything direct,' Philip said. 'He's just making use of things that come his way—he's not likely to do anything that can be traced directly to him.'

'I should think not,' said Derek. 'The whole thing's a fantastic idea, Torrington, if you don't mind my saying so. I don't want to be rude, but really I think you're imagining things. You write, don't you? Life isn't like books, is it?'

'Sometimes it is, and more horrifying and cruel than any book,' Philip told him. 'The whole key to this is character—a man like Dereham wouldn't marry a girl like Penelope just for the colour of her eyes.'

'I agree with Philip—I don't think it's fantastic,' said Betty. 'Penny was in a terrible state, quite ready to jump in the river, particularly if she thought she was a failure. And why didn't he tell her he'd left Automobile Kings?'

'Why, indeed?' said Philip. There was a pause and then he added: 'She'd be ashamed—if she began to find out what Dereham must be like—ashamed to have been so deceived.'

They all stared at each other, Derek not quite convinced, but the others clear that Penelope was in grave peril.

'I don't see how he rigged her falling down the stairs,' said Philip. 'Perhaps it was a real accident, but he might have arranged something. He could have frightened her with the car, even though there are lots of other black Humbers in London. I think he contrived the sickness, with something he found to his hand—if I can prove that there will be something to go on—something to tell the police. It's useless so far—it's all just an idea.'

'But he must be—he must be mad!' cried Betty.

'He must be a sort of maniac,' Philip agreed. 'One who thinks that only he matters. Lots of people are like that but they don't carry it to such desperate lengths. I've made enquiries about the doll, and I'm quite sure of where he bought it, and that he had it specially altered to look like Penny and got it dressed in a frock like hers.'

He paused, and Derek said again, 'You must have imagined it, Torrington.'

'I haven't,' Philip said. 'Do you remember Macbeth? Lady Macbeth went mad because she could not sleep. If you've ever had a long spell of insomnia you'll understand how that could happen—lack of sleep, and days filled with horror and insecurity.'

'And someone who isn't one of the world's toughies to begin with,' said Betty. 'Oh, what are we to do?'

'We must try and get some proof,' said Philip.

'We must try and protect Penny—get her away from him somehow,' said Betty. 'Can't we go to the police?'

'They'd think we were mad—like you do, you aren't convinced, are you, Swindon?' Philip said.

'You convince me, but the facts don't,' said Derek.

'Penny is suspicious herself,' said Philip. 'When I was making enquiries about the doll I discovered she had been doing the same thing. That means that probably a great many other things have happened that we know nothing about. There might be something to go on there. But I'm afraid that if Dereham realizes she has any other idea that he isn't all he seems to be he may—may contrive another accident, this time a fatal one. I just need time to try and get some proof.' He thought of the envelope in his pocket, containing the shreds of tea-leaves.

'There's the girl in the doll shop,' Derek said.

'Yes.' Philip looked at him. 'Someone was killed in that shop this evening. I came past when the police were going in. Someone in the crowd said a girl who worked there had been stabbed.'

'But you don't mean—it couldn't have been Vincent!' Betty said. Her face was white.

'It seems more than a coincidence,' said Philip. He went on grimly: 'He might have known that Penelope had been enquiring about the doll he gave her. He may have wanted to remove all risk of being connected with it.'

'But you knew he'd given it to her,' Betty said.

'Yes, but we thought he'd bought it in the King's Road, and that he just happened to see it and thought it looked like Penny, when it wasn't like that at all. He may have just seen it in the window of Bric-a-Brac, but he cut its hair and got it a new dress to make it more like her. Actually when you look at it closely it isn't so alike, of course, the features are too vague; but the effect from a distance is rather uncanny. He probably gave it to her just as an afterthought, to make her feel edgy. She was strung-up and a bit jumpy even before her aunt died, I thought. No wonder, married to him. It was all part of a long-term policy to make her afraid. Perhaps he planned to rig a more serious accident later; it would be easier if Penny was already in a nervy state. Or maybe he hoped she'd save him the trouble by doing something herself.'

'Oh no!' Betty gasped. 'She never would.'

'Well, if she was wretched enough —' Philip's voice tailed away. 'She wouldn't be responsible.'

'But the old lady, Penelope's aunt,' said Derek. 'I can understand that when he met Penelope first of all he soon knew she'd inherit a fortune—everyone in a village knows all about everyone else and it wouldn't be hard to discover that. But she wouldn't get the money until her aunt had died. All this doll business began before that. Dereham couldn't have known that Mrs Vandyk would die so soon.'

Philip looked at him. 'She wasn't a good risk,' he said slowly. 'It was well known that her heart was bad. But I think Dereham knew precisely when she would die.'

Derek and Betty stared at him.

'I think he arranged for her accident,' Philip said. 'It seems to be rather a habit.'

20

Girl assistant stabbed at counter ran the headlines in next morning's *Daily Scream* which Penelope read in the train on her way back to London.

Last evening as dusk fell and the streets were thronged with rush-hour traffic, C.I.D. men were called to the premises of Bric-a-Brac, Ltd., an antique and curio shop situated in the region between Piccadilly and Bond Street, ran the story below the large black capitals. *Death had come suddenly, without mercy, to blonde, attractive Valerie Drayton, 23, sole assistant. Her body, stabbed, was found slumped on the floor under the counter by Herbert Wadham (see left) proprietor of Bric-a-Brac Ltd. when he made his customary call to check the day's takings. He immediately telephoned Scotland Yard.*

Robbery is believed to be the motive for the crime. The till had been opened, and the contents, some hundred pounds, had been taken.

Friends of the murdered girl (above) said last night that she planned to announce her engagement to Mr Wadham, who is 39, very soon. Pale and distressed, Mr Wadham spent four hours last night helping detectives to fill in the details of the dead girl's life. The weapon, a narrow stiletto-type knife, is believed to have been left in the body. Full story on page 7.

Penelope felt a shiver of pity as she read the paragraphs. There was an enlarged photograph of the dead girl, laughing and carefree, taken while on holiday by the sea, reproduced across the top of the page. Her face was familiar. Penelope could not remember ever having been in to Bric-a-Brac, Ltd., but perhaps she had worked previously in some other shop where Penelope had met her across the counter. Morbidly she turned to page seven to read further details of Valerie Drayton's childhood in Pinner, and of 'our special reporter's' interview with her widowed mother. What a pointless, dreadful crime. Yesterday morning that girl had not known that it would be her last awakening. Was it really ordained that her life should be cut short so soon? If someone had not murdered her, would she have been run over or stricken by a fatal illness, Penelope wondered. What had Valerie Drayton accomplished in the years that she had lived?

Depressed profoundly, Penelope turned the page and tried to concentrate on the fashion news, which was more cheerful with the return of the waist. After her long, tranquil night's sleep she felt a different person. At this moment there was nothing specific for her to fear: she could ward off her apprehension till she must meet and recognize it. She was rested; she felt alive and vigorous as she walked down the platform at Waterloo and plunged below into the Underground.

She went, first, back to the house in Kensington, and at once she noticed that the doll had disappeared from the mantelpiece where it had been left. After a search upstairs she knew it was not in the house. Her ivory ship remained, safe, on the window-sill. On a sudden impulse she looked in her jewel box and found that her diamond brooch had gone.

Somehow it was not a surprise. She sat down and thought about it. Vincent had sold it, because he was out of work and needed money, though surely he had only to cash a cheque on their joint account. But he would not do that, if he was in difficulties, she told herself, trying still to cling to a last few illusions. But if that was so, why not ask for the brooch? Why take it, without a word?

She made herself a cup of coffee, frowning as she spooned the dried powder into the cup. Somehow today tea did not appeal to her. After she had drunk it, very hot and sweet, she changed into her best suit, put on a velvet beret and her beaver coat, and went out again.

She took a bus to Piccadilly, and alighted outside Swan & Edgar's. She walked swiftly along till she came to the premises of Automobile Kings, Ltd. It was an imposing establishment, with its large invisible window-panes, and its giant motor-cars displayed within. She drew a deep breath to give herself courage and walked boldly in through the swing doors. A willowy young man sprang to open them for her, and she said bravely:

'Good-morning. May I speak to the manager, please?'

The young man looked taken aback. She did not seem quite like an applicant for the post of telephonist which he knew had to be filled, nor yet did she look like a possible client.

'Well—madam, perhaps I can help you? Mr Venables is in conference, I think,' he temporised.

'I can wait,' said Penelope calmly.

The young man, who had gleaming black hair and a small toothbrush moustache, was impressed by her air of determination.

'I'll enquire,' he told her. 'Please sit down. What name is it?'

'Mrs Dereham,' Penelope replied, looking to see if this meant anything to him. But he seemed unmoved.

She sat down on a large sofa over which a tiger-skin rug was nonchalantly draped, and waited. He reappeared quite soon and led her into the presence of the managing director.

Mr Venables was a stout, bald man, sallow-skinned, with rimless glasses.

'Good-morning,' he said, bowing to her from behind his enormous desk.

Penelope waded across the yards of ankle-deep carpet which stretched before her. The office was large, and furnished sumptuously in light maple and cedarwood.

'Good-morning,' Penelope said, and swallowed nervously. Then she plunged, aware that Mr Venables was watching her with some astonishment.

'I came to enquire about my husband,' she said carefully.

'Your husband?' Mr Venables' surprised expression increased.

'Yes. He—I think he worked here,' Penelope said doubtfully.

Mr Venables' eyebrows shot up into where his hair would have been.

'Do sit down,' he said, coming round from behind his desk to push forward a black-and-white striped chair.

Penelope was glad to obey; her knees seemed to be made of jelly.

'Now,' he said. 'Do I really know your husband?'

'I think so,' Penelope maintained.

'Dereham, Dereham,' said Mr Venables to himself. 'Wait a minute—I have it. Tall, fair—a moustache?'

She nodded.

'Ah yes—he was in the showroom for a few months—saw us through the Motor Show and left before Christmas,' he said happily, pleased at remembering.

'Before Christmas?'

'Oh yes—I'm sure of that. If you'll excuse me a minute I'll tell you exactly when he did leave.' He flipped a lever on his desk and a disembodied voice replied at once.

'Let me know when Mr Dereham left, will you please, Miss Ellis?' he asked it.

While they waited he offered Penelope a cigarette, and when she refused, lit one himself. In a minute or two Miss Ellis came on the air with the information that Vincent had left on the 12th of December.

'Thank you.' Mr Venables flipped back the switch. 'Surely you knew that, Mrs Dereham?' he said.

'I—wasn't sure of the date,' said Penelope slowly. 'He—didn't tell me he'd lost his job.'

'Dereham left of his own accord, Mrs Dereham,' said Mr Venables. 'I remember it distinctly now. He had been very satisfactory—he knew a lot about cars and was a good driver when clients required to try out new models, and his appearance was good on the floor. I was sorry to lose him, but I recollect he said something about going into business on his own. He's been back once or twice enquiring about secondhand cars—I know he was interested in a Humber we had, and took it out on trial, but he didn't buy it.'

'Oh,' said Penelope. A Humber. 'I see. He was—you said he was a showroom assistant, like the man who brought me in here?'

'Yes—a salesman, if you prefer it,' said Mr Venables.

Penelope looked at the pile of papers that waited on his desk. This was how she had pictured Vincent at work. She rose, slowly.

'You're busy—I mustn't keep you,' she said. 'Thank you.'

Mr Venables rose too, a little at a loss because of the apparent futility of their conversation, but also conscious of the pile of work awaiting him.

'Nothing wrong, I trust?' he said.

She shook her head, defeated, and he was aware then that she was no older than his own daughter. Something pathetic in the droop of her shoulders moved him.

'You're sure there's no trouble? Nothing I can do?' he said earnestly. 'If Dereham wants to come back I could consider——?'

'Thank you, no,' she said. 'It was good of you to see me.' She held out her hand. 'Goodbye, Mr Venables.'

'Goodbye, Mrs Dereham,' he replied, and came round once again from behind his desk, this time to open the door for her. His mind abandoned her when she had gone: just for a moment he wondered what it could all have been about, and then his telephone rang and he forgot her.

It was half-past eleven. Penelope walked away and turned into Piccadilly. She crossed the road and went up Regent Street. She knew what she planned to do, but she had run out of courage and had to restore it first. It occurred to her that she was near the site of yesterday's murder, and morbidly curious interest drove her on to pass the scene of the crime. She was not the only spectator; a crowd of people, mostly women, were gathered outside the shop where two policemen stood on guard attempting to keep them moving past. Penelope stared at the windows. The blinds were down and the door barricaded.

'Poor girl, terrible shame, wasn't it?' said a woman in the crowd as they jostled along.

Penelope realized she was being addressed. 'Dreadful,' she agreed.

'Such a nice shop, it was, that Bric-a-Brac,' said her new friend. 'I used to like looking at them dolls in the window. Come past here on me way to work, I do, every day, and always stop for a look. Once I went in and she showed me some of the things, thought I might get one of the dolls for my Mavis's birthday, so nice they were, all in fancy dress, but far too dear for me. Five guineas.'

'Dolls? Did they sell dolls?' Penelope asked.

'Oh yes, dear, didn't you never see them? So pretty, and quaint they were, quite small you know, with plaits.'

'Plaits?'

"Yes—dark and fair—and made of china. You don't often see china ones these days. As that poor girl said, they do break easy, and Mavis would likely have dropped it if I had of got her one.'

'Yes—yes, she might have,' Penelope said. China, but with plaits, and fancy dress.

'Ah well—doesn't do to keep on—never know your luck, do you? Hope they catch him soon, the brute.'

'Him?'

'Why, the murderer, of course. Reckon it was one of those teddy boys. 'Tisn't safe to cross the road, hardly, is it? Never know when you'll be coshed.' The woman gave a shiver and pulled her shabby coat more tightly round her. 'Fancy killing a poor girl like that just for some money.'

'Terrible,' said Penelope.

She walked on up the road. Presently she came to an espresso coffee bar and went inside. She drank a cup of scalding coffee and ate a sandwich. Then she emerged again into the road. A newspaper vendor's board caught her eye, and she stopped to buy the early edition of the evening paper. The murder story was sprawled all over the front page, and Penelope returned to the espresso bar to read it. There were more details of Valerie Drayton's life and humble origins, and reports of harrowing interviews with the unfortunate Herbert Wadham and the bereaved mother. A paragraph stated that medical evidence declared that the weapon had pierced the heart, and that possibly the murderer had some knowledge of anatomy which had caused the blow to be struck so as to cause instant death. The blade had been driven down between the collar-bone and the top of the shoulder-blade. An uninformed assailant would have been more likely to have struck between the ribs. This indicated premeditation and that the girl had perhaps not been killed to prevent her giving the alarm over the robbery as had at first been thought. It was possible that the murderer had been a commando.

Penelope read the story through, dismayed at her own morbid fascination. When at last she left the coffee bar it was one o'clock.

She took a taxi to Sycamore Gardens and got out of it at the end of the quiet road. Plane trees grew behind railings that fenced in the gardens facing the row of shabby Georgian houses. The neighbourhood had seen better days. A small girl expertly twirling a hula hoop around her body as she walked along came past, face solemn and tongue protruding in concentration as she kept the plastic circle orbiting round her hips. Otherwise there was no one about. From the top of the road Penelope could see Vincent's Vauxhall outside No. 15. She walked towards it with as much purpose as the hula-ing child, mounted the steps, and rang the bell, deliberately keeping her mind a blank to defeat terror.

It was Clarrie who opened the door.

Penelope did not falter. She said clearly:

'Good-morning. We have met before, I believe. My husband is here. I wish to see him, please.' She might have been a duchess.

It was Clarrie whose composure flew. Her eyes turned, evasively, and her colour faded.

Penelope noticed at once that she wore on her mauve wool dress, if not her own diamond brooch, its twin, and as she looked at it Clarrie's hand flew to it. Penelope swallowed. Her mouth felt dry, and she was aware of the rapid, panicky thumping of her heart.

'His car is outside, I know he's here,' she said, when Clarrie did not speak.

At this the older woman regained some power of movement. 'Come in,' she said, and called shrilly, 'Vin, come will you?'

But Vincent had already appeared at the top of the stairs. With no light on his face Penelope could not see his expression as he looked down on them, but suddenly she was desperately afraid of him. What a fool she had been to come here! All her past experiences began to crystallise and to make a mountain of almost visible menace. She turned, but Clarrie had closed the door and stood between her and flight.

'What the hell are you doing?' Vincent said. He ran down the stairs, lightly and quickly, and stood towering over Penelope and glaring at her.

'I—Vincent, what's wrong?' Her voice caught in fright, and she wailed the words. 'Why did you leave Automobile Kings without telling me? Who's this woman? Come home.'

Over her head Vincent and Clarrie's eyes met. With an effort he turned on his charm.

'My dear, you haven't been well. Now what are you up to chasing about and spying on me?' He spoke mildly, and took her arm. 'Come and sit down.'

Penelope wanted to fling his hand from her. She managed to suffer it to remain.

'It's you who isn't well,' she said. 'Please come home and explain, Vincent. If—if you don't love me any more and want to marry—her—I'll divorce you, you can be free.' At the moment such a simple solution unfolded before Penelope like the gates of paradise. 'I always thought it was queer, you wanting to marry me,' she chattered on, beginning to shake now with nervous trembling.

'Yes, I think we'd better go home, Penelope,' said Vincent. 'Of course I don't want you to divorce me, what a silly idea. But then you've had a lot of silly ideas lately, haven't you?'

'What are you going to do, Vin?' Clarrie's voice was high and anxious, and even Penelope recognized the fear in it.

'My brooch.' Penelope had lost her head now, and could not stick to one line of thought. She swung round, free of Vincent's arm, and pointed at Clarrie. 'Did you give her a china doll too? Or perhaps that is my brooch, and you've given her my doll. Look out, don't go dropping it or you'll fall downstairs,' she cried. She began to laugh: she knew she was nearly hysterical, but control was almost out of her power. 'You tripped me off the bus, didn't you,' she accused Clarrie. 'You caught my heel with your umbrella. Was it so that you could be with Vincent if I was ill? I don't care why it was—I don't want him—you have him—I'll go away.' She began to go towards the door, and instinctively Clarrie moved away.

'Don't let her go,' snapped Vincent.

'Oh, leave her, Vin,' said Clarrie wearily.

'What, now? When we're almost home?' Vincent said. 'Not after all this, you bet. Come, Penelope. We will go home. You and I have an account to settle, haven't we? I've got to decide what to do about you now that you've become such a little busybody.' He caught hold of her wrist and jerked her towards the door. 'Get your coat, Clarrie, and see if anyone's about. And you, Penelope, you'll do what you're told or you'll be sorry. You'll be sorry anyway, of course, in time.'

She felt something against her ribs, hard, unyielding. Looking down in fascinated horror she saw that it was, in fact, a gun.

Then she remembered why Valerie Drayton's face was familiar. She was the girl who had spoken to Vincent in Bellini's restaurant.

21

It was one o'clock in the morning when Philip finished writing.

'You must get some sleep, Philip, truly,' said Betty, now in her dressing-gown, coming into the room where he sat at Derek's desk.

'She's right,' Derek said, getting up from the arm-chair where he had been sitting while Philip covered sheets of his writing-paper with neat, angular handwriting. 'You'll help no one if you wrap your car round a tree going down to Hampshire. Get in a few hours and then go off when it gets light in the morning. Penny's safe enough till then, we know that.'

'I suppose so.' Philip got to his feet. He did feel weary after his journeying up and down the length of the country; he had slept little in Edinburgh, and had started the day very early there with his expedition to the side streets of the city with Cartwright before his flight back. It was true that there was nothing to be done now till morning, so he agreed with his hosts and was soon in bed in the Swindon's spare room, in borrowed pyjamas. But sleep eluded him. He switched on the light and ran again through the pages that he had written, making sure nothing had been forgotten. Then he lay restlessly, wondering if it really was the true answer or whether he had in fact imagined the whole thing out of a chain of coincidence. Finally at last he dropped into a fitful slumber until Derek, tousle-headed, came to wake him as promised at six o'clock.

Half an hour later, having shaved with borrowed tackle and been fortified with tea and two boiled eggs, he was driving away through the lightening streets, out past the waking suburbs and on to the A.30 road, while Derek set off to see that the pages Philip had written the night before were delivered into the right hands.

It was nearly eight o'clock when Philip reached Foxbourne St. Mary. Towns and villages through which he passed were coming to life ready for the day; buses full of factory workers trundled down the roads, and in the suburbs cars began the daily procession citywards. Philip drove past the cottage where Kitty Francis lived, resisting the urge to go in: Penelope would still be asleep, very probably, and he could not begin to explain to her; he must find his proof first.

At Greyfriars he was able to let himself in easily with the spare key which Cartwright had elected not to return to Vincent. The house, empty and unlived-in, was cold and smelt damp. Condensation streamed down the walls and windows. Philip went upstairs and into the bedroom that had been Great-Aunt Hermione's. All the furniture was huddled under dust-sheets in the centre of the room. Philip discovered the wardrobe and looked inside. The electric fire was still there, where he had put it after the inquest. He did not touch it, but closed the door again. Then he went over to the fireplace. Soot had blown down the chimney and spattered the stone surround which was otherwise bare. Philip peered about, moving the largest lumps of soot gingerly with the back of his finger. He looked along the skirting, and then he pulled back the small Persian rug which covered the plain pile carpet in front of the hearth. There was no trace of what he sought, but there was a hole in the coffee-coloured Wilton. Years ago it had been burnt, and the rug placed above to conceal the damage. Philip wrapped his handkerchief round his hand and very cautiously put it through the hole. He felt about below. In a moment he withdrew his hand. Clasped in the handkerchief, he held a sixpence.

By the time he reached Kitty Francis' cottage Penelope had been gone for over an hour.

Philip leaped into his car and drove straight back to London. The miles flashed past: he had never driven so fast. He roared across the aerodrome at Blackbushe, fumed with impatience when he was held up at the level crossing in Sunningdale, and jumped the lights in Staines. When he reached the little house in Kensington he wasted no time in ringing the bell but immediately let himself in and rushed upstairs, heedless of traces he might leave this time.

Penelope was not there, and neither was the china doll.

He rang up Betty Swindon, who told him she had had no word of Penelope, but that she would stay in all day and if Penelope came she would keep her there, using force if necessary. Then Philip telephoned Derek, who reported the safe delivery of the papers entrusted to him. Then he rang up Scotland Yard.

After that Philip wrote a note to Penelope which he propped up on the mantelpiece where she would be sure to see it the moment she came in.

At twelve o'clock, as Penelope was entering the espresso coffee bar, Philip was admitted into Mr Venables' office at Automobile Kings Ltd. At a quarter to one, when Penelope was getting into the taxi that took her to Sycamore Gardens,

Philip went into the espresso bar she had just left, missing her by seconds. He ordered a sandwich and sat down to eat it. On his chair lay a crumpled edition of the evening paper, open at the page describing the latest events in the case of the murdered shop assistant. Philip quickly read it as he ate. Then he went back to his car; he did not know what to do: there seemed to be nothing that would retrieve the situation, and no course of action he could take. He returned to Kensington, but the little house was still empty and his note had not been moved. In the end he went back to the Swindons' house, but Betty had no news.

It was two o'clock.

'Let's ring up,' Betty said. 'She may have come in now. I think you should have waited there, Philip, not just left a note.'

'I do too,' he said wretchedly, 'but supposing that chap had come first—oh, hell. Yes, ring up. If she's not there I'll go back.'

Betty went over to the telephone, but before she could lift the receiver the bell started to ring. Betty answered it.

'Oh, my God,' she said, when she had listened to the voice at the other end of the line. 'Wait—Mr Torrington's here, you'd better speak to him.' She handed the telephone to Philip. 'It's Scotland Yard—you were right about the tea,' she said.

Philip listened intently to what was said to him. Then he said: 'Mrs Dereham's disappeared—she spent last night in the country as you know, but she left there to catch the eight o'clock train to London. She went to Automobile Kings in Piccadilly at twelve o'clock, and she hasn't been seen since. Yes, yes. Yes.'

He listened again while the crisp voice at the other end spoke.

'I was going there myself,' he said. 'But of course—yes, I will.'

Betty felt desperately sorry for him suddenly. He looked so young and vulnerable, his bright hair rumpled and his tie askew. He hated the inactivity of waiting for the next development before he could spring to help.

At last he put back the telephone.

'Let's ring her,' he said heavily, and began to dial the number.

22

The telephone rang and rang. Penelope sat staring at it. She wondered how the others could endure the persistent sound it was making. She started to count the number of rings: burr, burr; burr, burr; it went, and when she reached thirty Clarrie spoke.

'For God's sake answer it, Vin.'

'Let it ring,' he answered. He was still standing with his back to the room, holding in his hand the note in Philip's writing that had been on the mantelpiece when they entered the house. When at last the ringing ceased he unfolded it and read the message. Then he handed it to Clarrie.

'Who's this Philip?' she asked. 'Why does he want her to ring up this Betty so urgently?'

'Boy friend of Penelope's,' said Vincent. 'Nosey, probably.'

'Could he have noticed anything?' asked Clarrie. She seemed jumpy and tense, Penelope was able to notice, even in her own extremity.

'What could he possibly have seen?' Vincent said. 'Relax, Clarrie. He doesn't know anything. The only loose end is that fire. I haven't fixed it—couldn't find it after the inquest on the old trout.'

Penelope stared from one to the other of them dazedly. The last half hour was almost a blank in her memory. They had bundled her out of the house in Sycamore Gardens so quickly, one on each side of her, when no one was passing, and Clarrie had driven the car while Vincent kept the gun thrust against her body. She tried to keep her brain under control, but she could not get past the horror. This could not be happening to her. He was mad, he must be, as she had feared. Her only hope seemed to be to play for time, to keep calm, and either to humour him or seize an opportunity to escape if it offered. She could not wholly understand Clarrie's rôle.

At the mews the baker was passing when they drew up. Penelope moistened her lips to scream; Vincent would not shoot if she did, it was bluff. But though she opened her mouth no sound came out.

'My wife isn't well,' Vincent had said to the baker, and the baker saw Penelope's white face and clucked with sympathy. The picture of concern, Vincent had led Penelope into the house with his arm around her before the sympathetic gaze of the baker and closed the door. Now she sat, numb and powerless, waiting to see what they would do. Vincent had put the gun back in his pocket and turned the wireless on so that if she screamed no one would hear above the monotonous voices of the speakers in Woman's Hour. With two of them in the room to prevent her, she had no hope of reaching the telephone to summon aid. The brief exchange between them about Philip's note heartened her, however. He at least must be back from Edinburgh and might even come to the house, though probably not, as he wanted her to telephone Betty. What a curious request. Perhaps one of Betty's children was ill and she wanted help.

Longingly, she thought of Philip. If only he would come! Unless he did, it semed to Penelope that only an interruption of some magnitude would offer her a chance to escape.

The others were talking. She bent her attention to what they were saying.

'I'll have to go and fix it,' Vincent was saying. 'If that redhead has smelt a rat it's the only possible thing they could get on to. There's nothing to connect me with the other—no blood, I saw to that, leaving the knife in, and no witnesses. They'll never explain that one.'

'Oh Vin!' Clarrie was looking horrified. 'No!'

'Had to be done, Clarrie. She knew about the doll—spotted me the other night with the kid here. Might have made trouble, after. Photos in the papers—Kid Bride, and that. Best be safe.'

'But —' Clarrie turned her head away.

'Don't you get squeamish, now,' said Vincent.

'Let's cut,' Clarrie said. 'Leave the kid and let's clear out. Never mind the money.'

'Come on, come on, my girl,' said Vincent. 'We'll fix it, don't you worry. By tonight our troubles will be over. I'll take the kid down with me to Hampshire. We might manage another little electrical accident.'

Suddenly, horribly, Penelope knew.

'You killed Aunt Hermione,' she whispered.

'Top of the class,' Vincent said. His clipped, precise voice had altered in the last minutes; vaguely Penelope was aware that his speech had coarsened and grown careless. 'Let's say I helped nature on a bit,' he said.

'That shop girl—you did that too!'

Though she knew it was true, Penelope could hardly believe it.

'Vin—that girl—I don't like it,' Clarrie said. She was looking at him with an expression of horror on her face.

'She was expendable,' Vincent said. 'Got some money out of it too, not a lot, but it'll be a help in case we don't get all this other, though I think we're safe. I tell you there's nothing to worry about. We'll fix the kid, and scarper, and then we'll be in clover. Take it easy, Clarrie, don't lose your nerve now, after all we've done together.'

'Let's get away while we can,' Clarrie said. 'Never mind the kid or the money. We're in too deep this time.'

'We can't leave little Penelope,' Vincent said. 'She knows too much. Much too much.' He crossed the room towards her. His left hand was in his pocket. She could not look at him, she shrank away from him into the chair, hiding her face; this could not be happening. She had time for a moment's surprise when she felt the blow on the side of her head, and then she became unconscious.

23

She came round to find herself in surroundings that were familiar, but it was some minutes before she could identify them. Then she realized that she was lying on Great-Aunt Hermione's bed at Greyfriars. The room looked strange and spectral draped in dust-sheets, and it was very cold.

Vincent was moving about by the fireplace. She turned her head cautiously to watch him. He seemed to be searching for something. He turned back the hearthrug and probed about in the carpet underneath, as Philip had done earlier. Then he seemed to abandon the search. Penelope saw that the electric fire stood in the hearth, and Vincent now put his hand in his pocket and then appeared to be fitting something into the fire. She noticed, without really taking it in, that he wore gloves. In front of the fire, on the stone hearth, was an object that she recognized with surprise as the rubber mat out of the bathroom.

He turned and saw that she was watching him.

'I'm going to show you how your aunt died,' he told her, approaching the bed.

She closed her eyes. She knew he was completely insane and that he meant to kill her; and she did not see how she could hope to be saved.

'She got electrocuted, didn't she? Poor old thing,' said Vincent. His voice was rather high. 'I'm sure you wonder how.'

In spite of herself Penelope opened her eyes.

'Ah, that's better,' said Vincent. 'Too bad about the bump on your head—they'll think you hit it on the fireplace if I arrange you carefully. Yes, Penelope, you're going to electrocute yourself too, trying to find out how your aunt did. Get up.'

She remained where she was, motionless, and closed her eyes again. At least she need not make his task any easier, and she doubted if she had the strength to lift her aching head.

She had, however. He jerked her off the bed and dragged her across to the fire. She tried to struggle, clawed at him desperately with her hands and kicked, but she was too weak to make much impression on him, and he was too preoccupied to notice the blows she tried to strike. He got her arms behind her and forced her on to her knees in front of the fire. The stone of the hearth was cold under her stockings; Vincent himself had both feet firmly on the rubber mat. Penelope saw that a pair of nail scissors protruded from the element of the fire, wedged between the bars.

'No tongs for you—they've disappeared, so you took a pair of scissors to experiment,' he said. 'Of course, afterwards I will take the sixpence out of the fire and fix the earth again. No one will quite know what you touched. Now take the scissors, Penelope.'

He let go of her with one hand for an instant and pressed the switch in the wall. She struggled. There was no point in screaming, no one was there to hear her. She tore at him with her nails till he caught her hand again and forced it out towards the fire. Then she did begin to scream, as slowly, inexorably, he pressed it down on to the scissors and she felt the thin steel, cold, against her hand.

Cold.

She was not dead. There had been no terrible shock.

She ceased struggling and held the scissors, the screams dying in her throat. There was no heat from the fire.

Vincent swore and flung her from him. He moved to the plug in the wall, pulling off his gloves as he examined it and tugged at the flex. Then he thrust it back into its socket and caught hold of the fire.

Somehow Penelope got to her feet and staggered away across the room. Her hands, groping, met the stuff of his coat which was thrown across a chair. She felt a hard lump in the pocket, and acting more from instinct than reason took it out. It was his gun. As she lifted it in a wavering hand to point it at him, Vincent suddenly uttered a high, strangled scream, and crumpled on to the ground, over the electric fire, just as Aunt Hermione had done a few short weeks before.

The acrid smell of burning tweed began to fill the room.

24

'But how? How? I just don't understand,' said Penelope wearily. It was much later that evening, and she was lying under a rug on the sofa in Mrs Torrington's drawing-room, in front of a blazing log fire. Queenie and Cartwright were also in the room, sitting neatly side by side with hands folded on their laps. Dr Torrington, smoking his pipe, sat in a big armchair; and Mrs Torrington, her face filled with concern, sat at the end of Penelope's sofa holding her hand.

The memory of the last hours was a blur to Penelope. When she realized that Vincent was dead she had somehow staggered from the room, only to find the passage outside full of policemen. Somewhere among them had been Philip, and then Dr Torrington had appeared and had taken her away in his car.

The police had been at Greyfriars for hours, minutely examining the house and taking photographs. They had only now allowed Philip to leave and follow his father and Penelope home. He stood by the window with his back to the room, his hair sticking up untidily like a schoolboy's.

'Shouldn't Penny be in bed? She's taken an awful pasting,' he said at last, turning round.

'And so have you, my boy,' thought his father. Aloud he said. 'She'll rest better after an explanation, Philip. She's all right—just a bit of a headache, eh, Penelope?'

Penelope looked at him gratefully.

'Please tell me what happened, Philip,' she said.

'Well.' Philip smoothed his hair down over the crown of his head. He walked across the room to the fireplace, where he leaned against the mantelpiece, careful not to keep the warmth of the flames from the others. 'I don't quite know where to begin,' he said.

'At the beginning, please,' said his mother. She was completely bewildered by the impact of violence that had called her husband to Greyfriars so suddenly, from where he had returned bringing Penelope, grey-faced, hardly able to walk and with a bump like an egg on the side of her head. Since then, while Penelope dozed, waiting for Philip to come back, Dr Torrington had been raging about like an angry gladiator, refusing to explain; and now here was Philip, usually loquacious, turned into a silent shadow. She had no idea why Queenie and Cartwright were here; all she had registered was that there had been some sort of accident and Vincent Dereham was dead.

'It was the fire,' Philip said at last. 'Right at the beginning, on Christmas night. I knew there was something wrong but it took me all this time to realize what it was.' As long as he lived he would never, he was sure, forget that if he had only realized earlier what had happened Penelope would have escaped the weeks of anguish that had now ended, and but for a miracle would have also caused her death. He straightened his shoulders and went on.

'Aunt Hermione never curled her hair before going to bed,' he said. 'She'd therefore turned on the fire to get warm. So why did she touch the tongs? There was something odd about how she lay across the fire when we found her, too.'

'But if she had a heart attack—it was all gone into at the inquest,' said his mother. 'She fell across the fire.'

'But she was holding the tongs, and they were poked in between the bars of the fire,' said Philip. 'Her hand was doubled back across her body.' He paused for a minute, looking at them. 'I'd been talking to her before dinner; she'd asked me to put the tongs on the fire for her, and I'd left them straight across the guard, with the handle to the right. If she'd caught hold of them like that her own hand wouldn't have been across her body and bent back. The tongs had been moved by someone and poked in between the bars, and left with the handle pointing the other way because whoever moved them was left-handed.'

There was a little silence. Philip had a picture in his head of Vincent holding the sherry decanter in his left hand.

'He also rested a coin between the bars of the fire, where the current goes into the element, to touch the frame, so that the whole fire was alive with electricity as soon as it was switched on,' said Philip. 'That was what he did again tonight. And he had disconnected the earth terminal in the plug. It was to put the plug right that he came down tonight. I expect he'd already looked for the sixpence he used and failed to find it—he was peering about on the floor directly Aunt Hermione died. I vaguely noticed it, before he took Penelope out of the room. The sixpence must have got dislodged when Aunt Hermione fell on the fire. I found it yesterday on the floor under the carpet. I know Queenie would have found it anywhere in the room, when she was cleaning, if it hadn't rolled through a hole. It would have been very easy for Dereham to make out someone had dropped it.'

'But why?' asked Mrs Torrington again.

Philip said: 'Aunt Hermione was going to alter her will and leave me some of her money. Dereham must have known.'

'Yes, he did.' Penelope spoke at last. 'She told me too, and I told him.'

'We all knew Aunt Hermione's heart was bad. Dereham realized when he married Penelope that it would probably be just a matter of months—at the most a year. Then he saw that part of the fortune would disappear—so —' he stopped.

'So—he married me because of the money?' Penelope whispered.

Philip nodded. 'He ran into Major Tompkins quite by chance at a race meeting—more or less asked himself down to stay, met Penelope and discovered the setup,' he said. 'In fact he and Major Tompkins had only been together for a few weeks in Africa and really hardly knew each other.'

Penelope turned her head away and stared at the brocade cushion on the sofa, fiercely, till the tears that had rushed to her eyes departed. After a moment Philip continued.

'He planned the business with the doll. He bought it in London, altered it to make it look more like Penelope, and gave it to her. His—that woman made the dress for it, like one that Penelope had, and they cut its hair. At dinner on Christmas night he got Major Tompkins to tell the story about an African who died of fear, and we also all discussed voodoo and so on. That sort of conversation could have been contrived at any time, but he developed it then because he knew Aunt Hermione would die the next morning. It was a surprise to him when she died that night because he had not expected her to use her fire for warmth, knowing the house was efficiently heated by radiators. When he saw the body he did exclaim "What already?" or something like that.'

Philip straightened and looked down at the fire. 'He banked on Penelope being very upset by the death of her aunt, and so already in a slightly nervous condition. He put the idea into her head that fear could kill—or that a person could be doomed to die. You did think that, didn't you, Penny?'

For the first time he addressed her directly. She looked at him and nodded.

'Then you began to have accidents, didn't you? I know about the bus and the car and the stairs—I expect there were others, and you were sick, too.'

Penelope just nodded, once more.

'Vincent made you have the accidents,' Philip said, gently.

'That woman—Clarrie—she tripped me on the bus, didn't she?' Penelope said. 'With her umbrella? And it was Vincent in the car?'

'Yes,' said Philip. He looked at the others, whose faces were bewildered. 'I'll explain later—let's get Penny's side of it straight first,' he said.

'He borrowed the car from Automobile Kings. He probably wore glasses or some simple disguise to prevent you recognizing him. You didn't know he'd left Automobile Kings, did you?'

Penelope shook her head. 'I found out later,' she said.

'The sickness, then. I thought he might have given you something to upset you—but I couldn't really believe it—it was just a hunch because the doll seemed such an odd present and I knew he'd lied about it,' said Philip. He went on to explain the chance that had taken him past the windows of Bric-a-Brac Ltd. to see the dolls, and confessed to his prying in Vincent's desk where he discovered the fragments, without the dress, of the broken one.

'It was all really because I didn't like Dereham,' he said. 'There was nothing concrete to go on; I didn't see how he could make you sick—he wouldn't risk buying poison, I was sure. Then I realized about the tree. That one at the end of your road. I'd kept noticing it, and suddenly I knew why it worried me—it was a laburnum tree.'

'Oh, my God,' exclaimed Dr Torrington, covering his eyes with a hand.

'Laburnum seeds are poisonous, and in small amounts cause sickness,' said Philip. 'Isn't that right, Father?'

'Yes,' said the doctor. 'You get cases of children eating them and becoming ill.'

'Dereham crushed them and put them in the tea, Penny. We know that now,' said Philip. He knew she must hear the whole story, learn every detail, have time to face all it implied, and recover. Deception by omission would never help her; only truth, time, and at last, he prayed, he himself, could do that.

'When I was certain that he meant to harm you I tried to find some proof that he wasn't all he made out he was. I discovered that no one really knew much about him. Tompkins didn't, though everyone thought they were old friends, because Dereham had implied it. I discovered about Queenie and Cartwright having left, and I knew you'd never do a thing like that in such a heartless way; Dereham must have banked on you being too ill to find out, or hoped to convince you if you did that it was for your own good. He probably felt he had a powerful influence over you,' Philip said.

'He did,' Penelope said, and shuddered. 'Till I pulled myself together,' she added. Would she ever, she wondered, nerve herself to tell Philip about that moment on the bridge? Looking at him, with his hair ruffled, his funny amber eyes gazing so earnestly at her, realizing that but for him she would probably now be dead, Penelope knew that a day would come when she would be able to tell him every slightest detail; he cared enough to risk everything in saving her: he had believed in her when she had not believed in herself; he would understand, and not condemn. But that was in the future, not now.

'I went up to Scotland,' Philip was saying. 'I had to get hold of Cartwright and it was quicker to fly than write or wire. Queenie came back with me and he followed by road—after we'd had a talk we were all so uneasy that we felt we'd better all come down and be on the spot, though we hadn't a definite plan.

'Then you'd disappeared.'

Later, Philip would tell Penelope, and she would comprehend, all the agony of mind that he had known on her account, but not yet.

She said, 'I'd begun to find out. I came down here because I wanted to tell you, Phil. You were the only person I knew would understand.'

'Oh, Penny darling,' Philip said, forgetting the presence of his parents in the room. 'And I wasn't here when you wanted me. To think what might have happened!' He could not bear to do so, and a gruff cough from his father brought him back to the present.

'There was the tape, you see, and my mother.' Penelope was not really listening to him; she was frowning in an effort at concentration.

'Tell us, Penny,' Philip urged.

'Well,' she said, and swallowed. 'He told me my mother had committed suicide by taking sleeping pills,' she said at last, and looked gravely at the doctor. 'Did you know her, Dr Torrington? What really happened?'

Dr Torrington's face was thunderous.

'Your poor mother died because she had no strength to find the will to live, after losing your father two days before you were born, Penny. She was a fragile, delicate creature, and things were bad. She wasn't strong enough. But as for anything else—why, she was the sweetest, sanest, most clear-minded creature I knew.'

At these words Penelope visibly grew less tense, and she almost smiled in her relief. Dr Torrington, on the other hand, seemed about to explode with wrath and was muttering under his breath.

'Now the tape, darling,' Philip prompted gently. 'It was on the stairs, wasn't it? Tell us.'

She described her fall down the stairs, and the discovery of the tape and drawing pins in Vincent's dressing-gown pocket.

'I though he must be mad,' she said. 'At first I'd just thought he'd lost his job and was afraid to tell me. That was after I'd rung up Automobile Kings and found he wasn't there.' She told them then of her fears, and of her phone call. 'How he must have despised me,' she said, wonderingly. 'He was sure I'd be obedient and do nothing he'd forbidden.' She shivered, and Mrs Torrington murmured, 'Oh my dear! You were so young.'

But Penelope would not allow herself an excuse. She shook her head impatiently, and after a minute went on with her story. 'At last, after a very long time as it seemed, I realized he was mad, not me,' she said. Terrifying as the realization had been, it was still better than knowing her own wits had gone.

'But why didn't you tell us, my duck? Why didn't you?' Queenie, who had been sobbing quietly throughout the recital, now rushed across the room to Penelope, who raised herself upright on the sofa and sat erect and proud.

'I was married,' she said, with pathetic dignity. 'I had to stand on my own feet. I did come to Philip, in the end, but he wasn't here.'

Philip wondered if she would ever learn to forget her shame; sitting like that, stiff and straight, she might have been thirty and not a girl still in her teens. His mother was helping Queenie restore herself to order, and in the resulting general post about the room he discovered that he had taken her place beside Penelope, and was now holding her hand. He held it very gently, for she must never be afraid again, but he smiled at her encouragingly.

'Don't you despise me too, Philip, for being such a fool?' she said, her voice so low that only he could hear.

'Oh darling,' Philip said, and forgot his resolutions as he quickly kissed her hand, then hid it away in his again, beneath the rug.

'It's you I mind about,' she said hurriedly, and then went on: 'How could he know I'd go downstairs that night, when he'd put the tape across the stairs?'

'First he made you thirsty—put extra salt in the supper, or slipped you a travel sickness pill, they tend to dry your mouth,' said Philip. 'Then he hid the toothglass so that you'd have to go downstairs.'

'I did have very salty scrambled egg that night,' Penelope remembered. 'I noticed it—but he'd been so kind, I ate it up.' Her voice shook, but she did not cry. She dug her fingernails hard into Philip's palm and added, 'Of course, I'd been sick too; that always makes you thirsty.'

There was a little silence. The four oldest members of the party were finding the whole story so appalling that they doubted the evidence of their ears; but Queenie, always resilient, rejoiced at the sight of her Penny with Mr Philip at her side, where he always should have been, of course, and then there'd have been no need for any of this to have happened. Dr Torrington was thinking that his son, although so disappointingly not in medicine, had proved at least that he had wits, and the courage of his convictions; while as for Penny, tragic though it was, it might well have ended fatally; she would, he knew, recover now. Mrs Torrington was torn between horrified pity for Penelope, and pride and joy in her son; and Cartwright was perhaps the least disturbed of all, for he had never liked or trusted Vincent.

'That girl,' Penelope said suddenly. 'The one in the shop. He did it, Philip.'

'Yes, I know, love,' Philip said.

'Because of the doll? She knew he'd bought it there?'

'Yes. But he'd lost all reason by that time. He was still sure he'd get away with it, but he was afraid if anything did go wrong she might connect him with it. The woman—Clarrie—told us the girl had met you at Bellini's and recognized him. She couldn't take it—Clarrie couldn't —' Philip said. 'She wouldn't come down here and help him clear up his evidence on the fire. She stayed behind to pack up his belongings and the police got her, not long after Dereham had left with you for Greyfriars. She soon broke down and told the lot.'

'He was proud of it,' Penny said. 'He boasted.'

'Darling, he was mad,' Philip told her. 'Not at first, but in the last little while he developed the sort of conceit that thinks it can never be wrong—a megalomania, I suppose. If this hadn't happened to you and that girl, it would have been something else. They think he'd been mixed up in other rackets—drugs, and so on, before he saw this chance of getting hold of a lot of money. The Yard are checking, but they know already that he'd been in and out of dozens of jobs. He'd been a film extra, and a tailor's model. He had been in the Army, that part was true; but he'd never been near Harrow, in spite of the tie.'

And there was a whole lot more about him that Philip knew, but which it would not help Penelope to hear.

'My dear child, we must be deeply thankful that you've come out of it alive,' said Dr Torrington heavily. 'That's all that matters now. You must forget the rest.'

'But I don't really see how I have,' said Penelope. 'He—was going to kill me because I hadn't killed myself. Why wasn't I electrocuted too?'

Philip looked across the room at Queenie.

'If ever I have something to be glad of, it was that,' said Queenie firmly. 'It was much too good an end for him, though.' She clasped her capable hands on her bag and glared defiantly at them.

Philip faced Penelope again. 'Now your turn, Cartwright,' he said.

Cartwright cleared his throat. 'Well, Miss Penny,' he said, 'before we left Greyfriars, naturally we drained all the water pipes and turned off the electricity at the mains. We did not get the Electricity Board out to disconnect it, as we had no instructions.' He stopped speaking, and folded his lips tightly together in a thin line.

'So that was it,' said Penelope. 'But—but later? What happened?'

Philip said: 'I came on down to Greyfriars because it was possible you were there. The Yard people had found traces of laburnum in the tea samples I'd sent them, taken from your house. I wrote down all I could think of to explain what was happening, and about the doll, to give the connection with Valerie Drayton. I knew if I went myself they'd either not listen or keep me there for hours, but if they analysed the tea and found anything they'd take notice at once. Derek Swindon delivered the report and the tea early this morning.

'It was the local police who came here. When the Yard got Clarrie to talk they knew there wasn't much time. Of course, what Dereham intended to do wasn't clear, but it was obvious he meant—meant something drastic.' Philip stopped talking and looked about the room at both his parents, and then back at Penelope. Under the rug, he felt her hand move in his, but it did not leave his grasp.

'While the police and I were rushing in at the front door—we knew Dereham was there because his car was outside—the Cartwrights had come in at the back. They heard the police car coming, but Queenie had already decided to make a cup of tea, not knowing what was going on upstairs.' He paused. 'The Aga wasn't alight, as the house had been left empty.' Philip glanced across at Queenie again.

'She put the electric kettle on,' he said, 'and of course she switched the electric current on at the main.'

Printed in Great Britain
by Amazon

75110112R00112